The Cattaneos' Christmas Miracles

A family reunited for a Christmas to remember!

A life-changing letter

Millionaire Leo Baxter is shocked to receive a letter from his biological parents, but tragedy strikes before they get the chance to meet. Now he has two siblings who want to see him...

A long-lost brother

Sebastian and Noemi Cattaneo are in the Swiss Alps for their parents' will reading. With a multimillion-euro business at stake and a surprise in store, it looks set to be...

A Christmas to remember!

Can the most magical time of the year—and finding love along the way—give this family the miracles they've each been waiting for?

Find out in

Cinderella's New York Christmas by Scarlet Wilson

Heiress's Royal Baby Bombshell by Jennifer Faye

CEO's Marriage Miracle by Sophie Pembroke

All available now!

Dear Reader,

Christmas is my absolute favorite time of the year, and it's important to me to spend it with my family around me. I'm fortunate to have a close family, and both my own parents and my husband's parents live right around the corner from each other—so there's plenty of opportunity for festive fun!

I think the reason family seems to matter so much at Christmas is the feeling of love that fills the whole season. And family doesn't have to be blood relations, or the people we grew up with. Family, at Christmas and all year round, is people who love you, who want to celebrate with you and who make you feel that warm, welcome buzz of contentment and home.

In this story, Maria doesn't think she could ever find home again at Mont Coeur. And Sebastian doubts that his family will ever be whole again, after all the changes of the last year.

But Christmas is a time for miracles...

Love and mistletoe,

Sophie x

CEO's Marriage Miracle

—

Sophie Pembroke

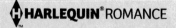
HARLEQUIN® ROMANCE

Recycling programs for this product may not exist in your area.

Special thanks and acknowledgment are given to Sophie Pembroke for her contribution to The Cattaneos' Christmas Miracles series.

ISBN-13: 978-1-335-13539-1

CEO's Marriage Miracle

First North American publication 2018

Printed in U.S.A.

Sophie Pembroke has been dreaming, reading and writing romance ever since she read her first Harlequin as part of her English literature degree at Lancaster University, so getting to write romantic fiction for a living really is a dream come true! Born in Abu Dhabi, Sophie grew up in Wales and now lives in a little Hertfordshire market town with her scientist husband, her incredibly imaginative eight-year-old daughter and her adventurous, adorable two-year-old son. In Sophie's world, happy *is* for ever after, everything stops for tea and there's always time for one more page...

Books by Sophie Pembroke

Harlequin Romance

Wedding Island

Island Fling to Forever

Wedding of the Year

Slow Dance with the Best Man
Proposal for the Wedding Planner

Summer Weddings

Falling for the Bridesmaid

A Proposal Worth Millions
The Unexpected Holiday Gift
Newborn Under the Christmas Tree
Road Trip with the Best Man

Visit the Author Profile page
at Harlequin.com for more titles.

This book is dedicated to Auntie Barbara Roberts, for always being my biggest fan.

CHAPTER ONE

MARIA CATTANEO—NO, she reminded herself, she was going by Rossi again now, even if it wouldn't officially be her name until after the divorce—gripped her son's tiny hand a little tighter as she stared up at the luxury chalet before her. How could something so familiar feel so strange at the same time? She'd spent Christmases and ski trips at the Cattaneo chalet in Mont Coeur for years—long before she and Sebastian had married—and on the outside, at least, the chalet had hardly changed a bit in all that time.

The same wooden veranda surrounded the oversized but traditional-style chalet, with festive greenery and berries wrapped around its beams in celebration of the season. A large green-and-red wreath hung on the front door. Inside, Maria could see lights twinkling through the windows, and knew that an absurdly huge Christmas tree would be decked out in red and gold, somewhere out of her line of sight.

Everything was the same. Everything, except her.

'Mamma?' At her side, Frankie looked up, his little face almost hidden by the hood of his snowsuit. It was freezing out, and darkness was falling; she needed to get him inside.

Which meant knocking on the door.

'Are you ready, *piccolo*?' Maria asked, forcing a smile. If Frankie sensed her unease and discomfort, he would only become distressed himself. And that wasn't going to make this enforced homecoming any easier on either of them.

'To see Papà?' Frankie nodded, his expression strangely set and serious for a two-year-old.

I'm glad one of us is ready, Maria thought, as she swept him up in her arms and climbed the steps. Then, with a deep breath, she knocked on the chalet door.

Maybe her sister-in-law Noemi would answer. Or even the mysterious new brother her husband and sister-in-law appeared to have acquired since Maria had left. Basically, anyone would be better than—

Sebastian.

The door swung open to reveal the familiar, muscular frame of her husband, and for a moment Maria was certain that nothing at all had changed. That she'd never left, that she was still in love with him, that they were happy…

She snapped out of it. *She* hadn't been happy. That was why she'd left.

Happiness was hundreds of kilometres away, back at the small cottage on the edge of her parents' estate, where she and Frankie had been living for the last year. It wasn't here, in the Swiss Alps, at the Cattaneos' luxury chalet. And it certainly wasn't with Sebastian, whatever her younger self might have hoped and dreamed.

He couldn't give her what she needed. If she'd thought for a moment that he could, there was no way Maria would have left at all. But the Sebastian she'd walked away from hadn't been capable of the love she needed. She had to keep that thought at the front of her mind this whole visit, otherwise there was just no way she would make it through with her heart intact.

When Sebastian had called and asked her to come for Christmas, with Frankie, her first instinct had been to refuse. Every other visit Sebastian had spent with his son, she'd managed to avoid, sending Frankie with his grandmother, or with Seb arranging to collect him from her parents' house when Maria was out. There'd only been two or three visits in the whole year, so it hadn't been hard to arrange.

But as difficult as it might be to go back, Maria also knew it was the right thing. Her son needed his father in his life. And Sebastian had been through so much lately…a Christmas visit from Frankie was the least she could do.

And then there had been that cryptic voicemail from Noemi on her phone when she'd landed, saying she hoped that Maria would be there to-night as she had something to discuss with the whole family.

As if Maria still counted as family. Even now.

Sebastian took a small step forward, and the light from the veranda illuminated his face. Maria held back a gasp, but only just. It had been twelve short months since she'd seen her husband, but from the weariness in his deep green eyes, and the lines forming between his brows, it could have been a decade or more. Sebastian had never really been the carefree, light-hearted sort—not like his sister Noemi—but Maria had never seen him looking quite so beaten down by the world before.

Was this because of her? She bit her lip as she waited for him to say something, but for a long moment he seemed content to just stare at her, and at Frankie, drinking them in. And she couldn't help but do the same, looking up into his once beloved face. His dark brown hair was cropped close to his head, shorter than she remembered it ever being before, and somehow it made him look even taller—although at six foot one he had always been almost a foot taller than her. She'd liked that, she remembered despite herself. Had liked resting her head against his chest and feeling his heart beat against her cheek. As if they had been connected in a way much deeper than the wedding vows their families had arranged for them to take.

This man had been such a huge part of her life for as long as she could remember. They'd grown up together, in all the ways that mattered. How could she have imagined she could cut him out completely, however far she ran?

'You came,' Sebastian said, at last, his deep voice reverberating through her body. Maria bit back a curse. She'd forgotten too how much just being near him, just hearing him speak, could affect her.

This was why she should have stayed away. But she had been unable to because…

'You asked me to.'

He gave her a small, uneven smile. 'That was by no means a guarantee that you would.'

Another sign of how little he'd really known her, Maria thought. If he'd understood how much she'd loved him once, he'd have known she could never have turned down that request. Not when he'd sounded so desperate.

'Please, Maria. I need you and little Francesco here for Christmas. Everything is different now. Please come.'

So, of course, she had. And at the back of her mind she had to admit that partly it was to see if 'different' meant what she'd always hoped it would. That their marriage could be what she'd once dreamed it would be.

Also because she still felt guilty—for leaving in the first place, and for not coming back sooner, when Noemi had first called with the terrible news.

'I almost came before,' Maria said, 'when I heard about your parents.' Salvo and Nicole Cattaneo had been second parents to her, too, and when she'd heard of their deaths in a helicopter accident in New York, Maria had thought she'd never stop crying. But, just like when she'd left Sebastian, she'd eventually straightened her spine and started over. The world didn't stop for grief, however much she might wish it would.

It couldn't have stopped for Sebastian either, she realised. He'd have been left dealing with not only the emotional fallout from his parents' deaths but also the practical side. Keeping the business—the world-famous Cattaneo Jewels—running like he always had would probably have proved a happy distraction from his grief, knowing Sebastian the way she did. But the news that he had a secret brother he'd never known about—one who, according to Noemi, had been left a controlling share in the family business—that couldn't have been easy for Sebastian to swallow.

She'd known how much he must be suffering, and her heart had ached for him. But still she hadn't been able to make herself return to Mont Coeur until Sebastian himself had called and asked.

After all, it was the first real sign she'd had that he'd even registered that she'd left him, that she hadn't just gone away for an extended holiday.

'Why didn't you come? For the funerals, at least?' Sebastian asked. There was no accusation in his voice, no implication that she should have been there, as his wife. Just normal curiosity.

She supposed she had to give him points for that.

'I wasn't sure it was my place. Any more.'

I wasn't sure you'd even notice if I was there.

'Maria.' Sebastian's eyes turned darker, even more serious, in the snow-lit gleam of the winter's early evening. 'There is always a home for you here. For you and for Frankie. Whatever happens. That much I can promise you.'

It's not enough. It had never been enough.

But if he hadn't understood that when she left, he wasn't going to suddenly get it now. Especially when he had so much other stuff going on in his life. So she said simply, 'Thank you.'

Sebastian turned his gaze to Frankie, whose eyes widened under the scrutiny. As Seb reached out to take him from her, Maria's hands tightened instinctively, even though her arms were aching from holding him for so long.

Frankie turned to hide his face against her shoulder with a tiny squeak of a whimper. She supposed she couldn't blame him. He'd only just turned one the last time they'd been here at Mont Coeur. His visits with his *papà* had been in Milan, close to the main offices of Cattaneo Jewels, or the villa the Cattaneos owned near her parents' estate. For all that the place and its people stirred up constant memories for Maria, for Frankie this must all seem so new and strange—and a little scary.

Seb's hand flinched away, the pain clear in his eyes.

'It's been a long day. We're both a little tired,' Maria said, trying to ease it for him, as she always had.

Seb's sad smile told her he appreciated the lie. They both knew that Frankie's real reluctance had far more to do with hardly having seen his father in a year, and then mostly on a computer screen, if Seb had managed to video chat when his son was still awake.

Maria forced the guilt to the back of her mind. It wasn't her fault that Sebastian had never lived up to his promise as a father—or as a husband. Just like she refused to feel guilty about leaving and seeking her own happiness.

How could she have possibly stayed, when

staying had meant accepting that the love of her life could never truly love her back?

Knowing that Sebastian had only married her because his father had told him to was one thing. Hearing him throw it in her face that awful night before she'd left was another.

'Come on, Maria. You knew what you were signing up for when you agreed to our fathers' plans. You married me to save your family business, just like I married you to get the merger between our companies. And now you're complaining that I'm spending too much time working at that same business?'

Except she hadn't, of course. Yes, she might never have gone along with her father's insistence on the merger if the family hadn't been in such dire straits. But she'd had other plans, other ways to save it—if only they'd let her.

Instead, she'd left her business degree, come home, and married Sebastian to give her family a physical stake in the newly merged business, taking the name Cattaneo as the name Rossi had disappeared from the company letterhead.

It hadn't been how she'd wanted to do it. But she never would have done it if she hadn't already been in love with Sebastian Cattaneo—and if she hadn't believed that one day he might come to love her back.

Accepting that the love she had given him so

freely and fully would never have been more than a convenience for him…that had been by far the bitterest pill to swallow. But swallow it she had—even if it had taken several years and a child to do so. She couldn't go backwards now, not when she'd worked so hard to move on.

'I'm sorry. I shouldn't be keeping either of you on the doorstep in this cold.' Sebastian stepped back, ingrained politeness obviously kicking in. He opened the door wider until the light from inside the chalet flooded out to encompass them all. 'Come in, both of you. Everyone's waiting to see you. And…welcome home.'

Maria's chest tightened just a little more as she stepped over the threshold. Mont Coeur could never be home again, even if she wished it could be otherwise.

As soon as Christmas was over, she and Frankie would be on their own again. Sebastian could keep the company—she had something far more important. Their son. And together she and Frankie would concentrate on building their own lives, far away from the Cattaneos and Mont Coeur.

And that was the best thing for all of them.

However much it hurt.

She'd cut her hair.

Seb was sure there were other changes in his

wife—and heaven knew he could see the incredible difference in his son, from the one-year-old baby he'd been when Maria had left to the two-year-old toddler in Maria's arms now.

But the only one he could focus on right now was the fact that she'd cut her hair.

Those long, long ribbons of jet-black waves that had hung almost to her waist were gone. Now her hair sat neatly on her shoulders, curled under at the ends. Still thick and glossy and vibrant as always, just…shorter.

And he was staring. He had to be, because Maria was starting to actually look concerned about him, which she hadn't been at any other point in the last year, not even when his parents had died and he'd acquired a new sibling out of nowhere and lost control of the business and—

Hell, now he was rambling. In his mind. Which he supposed was slightly better than doing it out loud.

What had happened to the calm, collected businessman he'd been a year ago? Oh, yes, his entire life had unravelled, that was what.

And it had all started the day he'd come home to find Maria packing sleepsuits and her favourite pyjamas into the suitcases he'd bought for their honeymoon years earlier.

'Sebastian?' Maria placed Frankie on his feet on the floor as Seb shut the door behind them.

Across the large, open living space of the chalet stood his sister and surprise brother, along with their new partners. More new people in his life to replace all those he'd lost.

But he wasn't ready to share Maria and Frankie with them just yet.

Maria began stripping off Frankie's bulky snowsuit. But her questioning eyes stayed on Seb, and he felt the weight in them.

'You cut your hair,' he said, with an apologetic half-smile. 'It suits you.'

'My life now suits me,' she said simply. The life in which she avoided him at all costs, managing to be elsewhere even when he arrived to collect Frankie from her parents' house. That life.

He was so glad it suited *one* of them, at least.

Then, as Frankie—free from his confining winter wear at last—wriggled free of his mother's grasp and took a couple of steps forward to investigate the antique nativity crib scene set up on a console table, Maria straightened and looked him in the eye.

'I want to be clear about one thing,' she said. 'Before we join the others or unpack or settle in or anything.'

Sebastian ignored the growing feeling of dread in his stomach as she spoke. 'Go on.'

'This is a visit. Nothing more. Once Christmas is over, Frankie and I will be heading home again, back to my parents' estate.' The emphasis she'd placed on *home* cut deep. This had been one of her homes once.

He had been her home.

'We're not staying, Sebastian,' she went on. 'I want that understood from the start.'

Seb forced a smile. 'Of course.' Maria's expression relaxed, and he knew he should leave it there, that to push it further would only ruin the fragile peace they seemed to have achieved.

But he couldn't help himself. He always had to try a little harder, a little longer. That was who he was. Who his father had raised him to be.

Oh, Papà, I wish you were here now to tell me what to do.

'But if you change your mind,' Seb said, ignoring the look on Maria's face, 'I wasn't just being polite when I said you always have a home here.'

'Seb…' Maria groaned.

'I know Noemi would love to have you around more. She misses you.' They'd always been close, his sister and his wife. He'd taken it as a sign that Maria was a rightful part of his family, as much as any of them.

But now Maria had gone and they had *Leo* in her place, which, as much as he'd reached a sort of truce with his unexpected brother, wasn't at all the same thing.

And apparently he'd said something wrong

again, as Maria had frozen and was staring point-edly at where Frankie was about to denude the stable of sheep.

'I miss Noemi, too,' she said stiffly. 'We should go and say hello.'

Then, without looking back, she crossed the room with swift steps and removed Frankie from the antique ornaments, and carried him over to where their family was waiting instead.

At least she missed one of them, Seb supposed. It was too much to hope that she might have missed him, too, when she'd made it so clear she didn't. If she had, she'd have wanted to see him on one of his few visits. The same way he'd spent them hoping to get just a glimpse of her.

Noemi rushed forward to greet them, a huge smile on her lips, and embraced Maria immediately. Sebastian trailed behind, watching as his wife greeted his sister with considerably more enthusiasm than she had greeted him.

Then Noemi knelt down in front of Frankie. As he moved to their side, Seb could see that his son's eyes were wide as he glanced around the large room and all of the people that he didn't know. Including his own father, it seemed.

'Hey, Frankie,' Noemi said, trying to gain his attention. When he looked at her, she said, 'Can I have a hug?'

Frankie glanced up at Maria, apparently for permission.

'It's okay,' Maria said.

That was all it took for Frankie to release his mother's hand and let Noemi draw his little body to her. 'I'm so happy you're here. I've missed you tons.'

Seb's heart felt heavy in his chest. Maybe Frankie didn't truly remember his aunt Noemi either, but he'd still allowed her to hug him.

He'd been almost *afraid* of *him*. How could he have let that happen? He'd hoped his visits and video calls would have kept his memory fresh in Frankie's little mind, but apparently they hadn't been enough.

And Seb knew that those few stolen days hadn't been anywhere near enough for him. He'd missed so much already. How could he let Maria go again, knowing how much more he would miss? Just like his own parents had missed Leo's childhood when they'd sent him away for adoption.

Frankie pulled back and returned to his mother's side, and Noemi stood again, turning her attention back to Maria.

Unable to watch any longer, Seb moved away to join Leo and the others. Hopefully Noemi would get to the point of whatever it was she'd called them all there to talk about soon, and then he could pour himself a large drink and feel depressed about his life choices again. That was always a good time.

'Noemi,' Sebastian said, 'why did you call us all here? We weren't supposed to meet for another week. Is it the attorney? Does he have news for us?'

Noemi shook her head. 'This isn't about the will.'

'Then what is it about?' Sebastian's gaze moved to the man who had his arm around his sister, and then back to Noemi. 'You know I don't like guessing games.'

A sharp elbow in his ribs told him that Maria had come to stand beside him. Oh, good. She'd retained one wifely habit at least.

'Maybe we shouldn't be here,' Leo said, presumably meaning him and Anissa.

'Of course you should,' Noemi said. 'You are my brother as much as Sebastian is. Our separation as kids was a horrible mistake, but I hope that in the future there will be no distance. Because I'm going to need all of you.'

Oh, God. What now? How much more disaster could this family take?

But then Noemi smiled. 'It's nothing bad. I promise. I... I'm pregnant. You're going to be uncles.' And then glancing at the women, she added, 'And aunts.'

For a moment there was silence as everyone took in the news.

His little sister. A mother.

'And we're having twins,' Noemi added. As if one baby wasn't enough of a shock.

But she was still his sister. Stepping forward, Seb stared her in the eye and tried to think what their father would have said. Salvo Cattaneo had always known what to say.

'Are you happy?' Because, in the end, that was what mattered, wasn't it?

Noemi smiled at him. 'I've never been happier.'

He studied her face for a moment to make sure she was telling him the truth. And then he put his hands on her shoulders, like he remembered their father doing. 'Then I am happy for you, too. Congratulations.'

He pulled her into his arms and gave her a tight hug—something he wasn't sure he'd done since they'd learned of their parents' deaths. His relationship with Noemi hadn't always been without tension or frustration but he *did* love her, even if he didn't always understand her, or what she wanted from him.

When Sebastian released her and backed away, Leo stepped up to her, and Seb watched to see how the new brother would deal with the news. 'You do know that I have no idea about children or how to be a cool uncle, right?'

She smiled and nodded. 'I think you'll figure it out. In fact, I'll insist.'

She reached out and hugged him, too, which seemed to take Leo by surprise.

When they pulled apart, Noemi moved to Max's side. She placed her hand in his, lacing her fingers with his. 'Do you want to tell the rest?'

'You're doing fine,' Max replied, sounding laid-back about the whole twin situation. Really, at this point, what more news could there be?

'First, I should probably introduce Max by his proper name,' Noemi said. Sebastian frowned. 'I'd like you to meet Crown Prince Maximilian Steiner-Wolf. He is the heir to the throne of the European principality of Ostania.'

A prince? His baby sister was pregnant by a *prince*? Seb knew he'd been distracted lately, but how had he missed this much?

Noemi drew in a deep breath and then slowly expelled it. 'And he has asked me to marry him.'

Well, that was something, otherwise Max and he would have had to have words.

Then Maria said, 'You'll be a princess,' and the reality of the situation set in fully. His wife always saw to the heart of a matter first.

'Wow,' Anissa said in awe, which pretty much covered Seb's thoughts on the subject.

'Yes, she will.' Max spoke up. 'She will be the most beautiful and compassionate princess. And

I couldn't be luckier. I promise you that I will do my best to make her happy.'

Sebastian looked between Noemi and Max. 'So you're moving to Ostania?' He wasn't sure how he felt about her being so far away. On the one hand, maybe they'd argue less. On the other, without Maria, and with his parents gone, and no commitment from Leo to hang around past Christmas, Seb would be on his own. Completely alone, for the first time ever.

His head spun at the thought.

'I'm afraid that my duties are increasing and after Christmas I will need to spend the bulk of my time in Ostania,' Max explained. 'I'm sorry to take your sister away from you all, but you will always be welcome at our home.'

'Don't you mean your palace?' Maria asked.

Max nodded. 'Yes. And it has a lot of guest rooms.'

'Guest rooms that I expect all of you to use regularly,' Noemi said firmly. 'Wait until you see this place. It's beautiful. And they have great skiing. But I wanted you all to know that we will be here for Christmas. It'll be a family Christmas just like Mamma and Papà would have wanted.'

With all them together—including Maria and Frankie. Even if it might be the last time it ever happened.

No. He wouldn't let that happen. He couldn't.

He had to fix things. And without his *papà* there to guide him, he was going to have to figure it out on his own.

'Now you all know everything, we can concentrate on celebrating,' Noemi said, clapping her hands together. 'Max, I haven't even properly introduced you to Sebastian's wife. This is Maria.'

'Mrs Cattaneo,' Max said, with princely suaveness as he took her hand.

'Not Cattaneo,' Maria said, too fast. 'I'm going by Rossi again now.' Wait. She'd given up his name now, too? They weren't divorced; legally she was still a Cattaneo. But the fact that she'd chosen her maiden name over his stung. Even worse was the way she'd said it so matter-of-factly, as if it were obvious.

Sebastian shot her a look. 'Did we get divorced without me noticing?'

He saw Maria's temper flare in her eyes. Good. He shouldn't be the only one angry here. 'Given everything else that happened in our marriage without you noticing, it wouldn't surprise me,' she said caustically.

'And now it *definitely* feels like a proper family Christmas.' Noemi rolled her eyes. 'Come on, Maria. Let's go show Frankie the master suite. I've had them set up the second bedroom there for the two of you.'

The second bedroom? Something primal rose

up in Sebastian's chest at the idea. Maria was *his* wife, and he wanted her back where she belonged, in his bed. In his arms.

Was that so much to ask?

His objections must have shown on his face because Noemi arched her perfect eyebrows at him in amusement.

'What?' Noemi asked her brother. 'You didn't really think she was going to just move back into your room, did you?'

Yes, of course he had, when he'd let himself think about it all. Which hadn't been often. He hadn't truly believed Maria would come home until he'd opened the door to find her standing there with Frankie.

But he'd hoped. And when he'd hoped, this hadn't at all been the homecoming he'd imagined.

'Frankie can stay here with me,' he said softly. Another wish he'd had dashed this evening—a joyous reunion with his son.

He hadn't thought it possible to miss such a little human as much as he had. But now it seemed that Frankie barely even knew who he was.

'Frankie wants to see his room,' Noemi said, sweeping aside his suggestion. 'Don't you, Frankie? Come on. You come with Auntie Noemi and Uncle Max and leave Papà to sulk here alone.' She put one arm around Maria's waist, guiding Frankie forward with her other hand until he stumbled. Maria swooped down to pick up the little boy, laughing and kissing him as she did so.

None of them looked back at Sebastian.

And then they were gone, his whole family disappearing through the door in a whirl of excitement and leaving him behind.

Leaving him alone.

Again.

CHAPTER TWO

MARIA KNEW SEBASTIAN probably better than anyone in the world, even—or perhaps especially—his sister. And she was almost certain that slipping back neatly into his life, into his bed, was *exactly* what Sebastian had expected. That she'd give up her little rebellion now she'd remembered what she'd walked away from. Or that she'd have forgotten the arguments, and the loneliness, that had made her leave in the first place.

Well. The bedroom situation was only the first of many disappointments he was likely to experience during her visit, then.

'Are you okay?' Noemi whispered in her ear, quietly enough that Frankie—who was playing a peek-a-boo game with his new uncle Max—wouldn't hear.

Maria nodded, not trusting herself to tell the lie aloud.

Of course she wasn't okay. She'd never be okay as long as she was here.

How could everything have changed so much? A new brother in Leo—and soon a sister-in-law, too, given how he was looking at Anissa—Noemi becoming a princess and mother to twins… And yet in some ways nothing had changed at all.

Not when it came to Seb, or their marriage, anyway.

Noemi sighed. 'My brother is such an idiot.'

Maria didn't argue with that.

The main staircase in the chalet wound up to the second floor, all warmth and wood and local charm. 'Chalet' was a ridiculous word for the Cattaneos' home in the Alps, in Maria's opinion. A chalet sounded like a small cosy wooden cabin or a rustic lodge you stopped in just long enough to grab a hot chocolate before heading home to a *real* house.

The Cattaneos' chalet was neither small, cosy nor rustic. It was huge, spanning four floors with sprawling bedrooms with balconies, large, welcoming living spaces, a well-appointed kitchen and huge dining room for entertaining. Not to mention the heated indoor Olympic-sized swimming pool in the outbuilding.

Maria's parents had always been wealthy enough—their own business portfolio had seen to that—but next to the Cattaneos they were paupers. And when their own business had gone through a difficult time—to the point of possible bankruptcy—well, it was no wonder her father had been so keen to marry his only daughter off to the Cattaneos' only son and heir, in a merger that could not only save them but strengthen *both* their companies.

In her father's mind, Maria had been nothing more than a means to an end, she realised now. While she'd been away, studying business, discovering a flair and aptitude for it that had surprised even her, he'd been making other plans for her future. His only child, his heiress—but only if there was a business left to inherit.

Except, while she was still an only child, Sebastian was anything but. Even if she discounted Noemi—who not only had no interest in the family business, according to Sebastian, but was now apparently running off to be a princess in Ostania, wherever that was—there was Leo to take into account, too.

It had taken a lot of questions to get the full story of Leo's existence from Noemi. Maria's father had returned from Salvo's and Nicole's funerals with news of a rumour—another Cattaneo child—and had demanded that Maria stop sulking and call her husband to find out the truth of it. She hadn't, of course. She'd called Noemi instead.

It seemed that Salvo and Nicole had conceived a son together, out of wedlock, when they had been only teenagers. Their families had been scandalised and, never imagining that the couple would actually stay together, had demanded that the baby be given up for adoption.

But once they had been free of their parents' oppression, married to each other and still madly in love, Salvo and Nicole had searched for their lost son. Even after they'd had Sebastian and Noemi, for more than thirty years they'd searched. And finally they'd found him—only for them to be killed in a helicopter crash on their way to see him.

It was tragic. Heartbreaking, even.

But the only thing Maria's father had taken away from the story was that there was another Cattaneo heir now. One who, if reports were correct, had been left a controlling share in the hugely successful jewellery business.

'Maybe you were right to leave him after all,' Maria's father had said, when he'd heard the story just a few weeks ago. 'The divorce settlement should be good, and you're still young enough to marry again. We'll choose better next time.'

Maria hadn't spoken to him since.

'Here we are!' Noemi's bright and cheerful tone caught Maria by surprise, and she almost slipped on the final step leading up to the top floor.

Sebastian's floor. The one they had shared ever since their marriage. Salvo and Nicole had taken one of the smaller suites on a lower floor, smiling knowingly as they'd declared that Seb and Maria might 'need the extra room' up there sooner or later. Preferably sooner.

This particular reason probably wasn't what they'd had in mind.

She bit her lip. How could she move back in here, even into a separate bed, and pretend that things were different? That she didn't still love her husband—and he wasn't still so indifferent to her?

But Frankie was excited to see his room and, one small hand in his aunt Noemi's, he'd barrelled on through to find out where he would be sleeping, Uncle Max chuckling as he followed behind.

Imagining their future probably—his and Noemi's. Noemi's baby bump was still relatively small, but it was there—as obvious as her excitement at starting a family with the man she loved.

And she did love Max, Maria could tell. And he loved Noemi—that was clear in every look, every smile he gave her. They would live happily ever after, just like Maria had once imagined she and Sebastian would.

How foolish she had been. Foolish, young and naive.

She knew better now, at least.

Sucking in a deep breath, Maria trailed after the others through the large open living space to the second bedroom—pointedly ignoring the archway that led to the main bedroom and the king-sized bed she remembered so well. The one where Frankie had actually been conceived, now she thought about it…

Except she wasn't—thinking about it, that was. That way madness lay.

'Well, what do you think, Frankie?' Maria asked, forcing a smile for the sake of her son. 'Will the chalet be a fun place to spend Christmas?'

Frankie, already bouncing on one of the twin beds, nodded excitedly. 'And with Papà and Auntie Noemi and Uncle Max?'

'Of course!' Maria took his hands in hers to try to calm the bouncing. 'And with Uncle Leo and Aunt Anissa, I suppose, too?'

Noemi nodded. 'We hope so, anyway. It was Mamma and Papà's last wish—to have all their children around the table for Christmas.' Her permanent smile turned a little sad. 'I just wish they were here to see it.'

Max wrapped an arm around her shoulders, holding her close against his side, and despite her best efforts Maria felt a pang of jealousy run through her. When had Sebastian ever instinctively comforted her like that?

Never. Because that would involve understanding what she was feeling. And Seb had never drawn his attention away from the family business long enough to even *try* to do that.

She looked away, but apparently not fast enough. Noemi, obviously having caught her expression, stepped out of the circle of Max's arms, looking concerned.

Max looked between them. 'Frankie, how about you and I go downstairs and explore the kitchen? I think I saw some delicious-looking Christmas cookies in there earlier.'

Frankie's eyes widened at the mention of sugary treats.

'If that's okay with your *mamma*,' Max added, too late for her to possibly say no.

Maria felt a tightening around her heart, and it had nothing to do with Frankie eating too much sugar before bedtime. It had been just the two of them for so long now that the idea of being separated—even just by a few floors—felt strange.

'We're all family here,' Noemi murmured, taking Maria's hand and squeezing it. Her sister-in-law always had been too good at reading her. 'And Max needs the practice anyway.'

Maria gave a stiff nod, placed a kiss on Frankie's cheek, and watched as Max swept the toddler up into his arms, already talking about chocolate chips and candies baked into cookies.

'He'll be fine.' Noemi squeezed her hand one more time before dropping it.

Maria sighed. 'I know.'

'The more important question is, will you?' Noemi asked.

Sinking down onto the bed, Maria covered her

face with her hands. Would she? Would she be okay, spending Christmas with the husband—and family—she'd left behind?

'I have no idea,' she admitted.

Alone.

Seb watched Maria and Frankie walk away, and felt the terrible word echoing around his mind. Through his heart.

Frankie hadn't even known him when he'd answered the door, had shied away from him when he'd tried to hold him. He'd wanted to video call more often, but it was always so hard to find a time during his son's waking hours. Maria didn't even bother answering if Frankie was already asleep, usually sending a text later to explain.

But, looking at his son now, Seb wondered how he could ever have imagined that ten minutes of video once every week or so could *ever* be enough. The baby he'd held in his arms last Christmas had gone for ever. When Maria had left, Frankie had only just begun to crawl—now he seemed to run everywhere on sturdy legs that were nothing like the podgy, squidgy baby ones he remembered. Even in the four months since he'd last visited, Frankie had grown so much. His eyes were the same bright hazel as in the photo on his desk, but they no longer gazed trustingly up at him. Instead, they were puzzled, even wary.

As if he didn't know Sebastian, his own *papà*, at all.

Seb clutched at the back of the nearest chair to steady himself. How had this happened? How could he have missed so much? And how could he ever get that time back?

You can't.

The voice in his head sounded like Maria's, like the day she'd left.

'You can't understand,' she'd said that day. 'You're not capable of it. I see that now.'

Capable of what? he'd wanted to ask. But she had already gone, leaving him behind to deal with the business, and his family, and everything else that fell on his shoulders.

But none of it, he realised suddenly, mattered as much as the year he had lost. A whole year of his son's life that he could *never* get back. Never experience as a father should.

That realisation hurt a thousand times more than learning that he had an older brother, that his parents had lied to him his whole life by never telling him about it. Hurt a million times more than learning that they'd left Leo the controlling share of the company that should have been his.

Hurt almost as much as hearing Noemi sobbing as she'd told him their parents were dead.

His parents were gone, soon Noemi would be disappearing with Max to wherever on earth his tiny country was, Maria would take Frankie away again, and all Seb would be left with was Leo—the brother he'd only discovered existed a month or so ago. And even he would probably head back to New York, and take the company Seb had given up his whole life for with him.

How had his life unravelled so completely in so little time?

Seb could feel it, spiralling out of his control, spinning his mind in tight circles until his head ached from trying to understand it all. His heart was too heavy in his chest, beating a sluggish, determined rhythm, reminding him that he, at least, still lived—even if his parents didn't. That he still had a job to do, even if the one he'd expected had been taken away. That he still wanted, and felt, even loved—even if his wife had left him and his son didn't recognise him.

God, Frankie. *Maria.*

He needed air. Cold, shocking, numbing air.

Good job he was in Mont Coeur.

Letting go of his support sofa, Seb staggered to the door and flung it open, gulping in the icy breeze as it hit his face. Then he stepped through onto the veranda, and stared out at the darkening mountains.

There was a whole world out there. So why did it feel like his had disappeared for good?

'Sebastian?' Leo's voice came from behind him

as he joined him on the veranda. 'Are you okay? You look… Is it Noemi's news?'

Seb barked a laugh. Noemi, his baby sister, a princess. A pregnant princess, at that.

At least one of them had gone after the life they'd wanted and had found it.

No, two of them. Leo seemed almost offensively happy with his new girlfriend, Anissa. They'd shared secret smiles and small touches and whispered jokes since they'd arrived, too, just like Noemi and Max. So clearly a pair, a couple—in a way he and Maria never had been. No doubt Max and his sister would be settling into what had once been *his* master suite in the chalet with babies and joy, taking over his home as easily as Leo had taken over his business.

'Okay, look, why don't we sit for a moment?' Leo's voice, calm and soothing, made Seb feel instantly guilty for his thoughts. As much as Seb resented being pushed out of the family business, even he had to admit it wasn't Leo's fault. He couldn't blame his brother for the circumstances of his birth, the lies their parents had told, or even the will they had left behind them.

Much as he might wish he could.

Seb was a logical, rational man. He had to be, to be a success in his business. His father had instilled in him from birth the weight of expectation, the obligations Seb had to his family. And

Seb had given everything he could to live up to them. He'd worked hard, done everything that had been asked of him.

And still it hadn't been enough.

Not for his father, not for Maria, not for anybody.

He wasn't enough.

Leo's arm over his shoulder was a heavy weight leading him to the wooden bench on the veranda and pressing him down onto it.

Maybe if he'd had a big brother all along, rather than discovering him at the age of thirty-two, things would have been different. But he hadn't.

'Do you ever feel like your whole life is unravelling in front of you, and you can't move fast enough to piece it back together?' His voice didn't even sound like his, Seb realised. Too low, too raw. Too desperate.

But Leo just laughed, a darkly amused sound Seb hadn't heard from him before.

'What do you think?' Leo asked. 'I spent my whole life thinking that no one wanted me, that my own parents had thrown me away, only to discover one day that they'd been searching for me almost my whole life. And then, when I was ready to meet them, they died before I got the chance.'

'And you got stuck with me and Noemi instead.' Yeah, that must have been a pretty big let-down.

'Actually, I kind of think of the two of you as an unexpected bonus. A silver lining maybe,' Leo said, and Seb looked up, surprised.

'What do you mean?'

'Well, I thought I'd lost any chance of ever having a family. Then I came here and met you two, and then Anissa…and now there's Max and Maria and Frankie, plus Noemi's babies. Suddenly I have more family than I know what to do with.'

'Maria and Frankie aren't staying.' Seb's mood dropped again at the reminder.

'Ah.'

'Yeah.'

Leo stretched his legs out in front of him, leaning back against the bench. Almost unconsciously, Sebastian followed suit. Leo's legs were longer than his, he realised, even though they were more or less the same height. Yeah, being the little brother really was going to take some getting used to.

'Do you remember what you told me when I called you from New York?' Leo asked, after a long moment of silence.

Seb tipped his head back and tried to remember. It had only been a handful of weeks ago now, but somehow it felt longer. Like his whole world had shifted again since then, with everyone coming home to Mont Coeur.

Leo had been in New York with Anissa, wooing her, or whatever it was that smooth, American-raised secret older brothers did. But he'd screwed it up—Seb had to admit that slight sign of fallibility had made it easier to warm to Leo—and Anissa had run when Leo had asked her to stay with him.

'I told you to wait,' he said finally.

'You said that if I loved her, I had to give her space and respect her decision,' Leo corrected. 'That I had to let love decide what happened next. And that I should let Anissa come back to me—if she wanted to.'

'And she did, of course.' And now they were blissfully happy. Good for them.

'So did Maria,' Leo pointed out. 'I mean, she's here for Christmas, isn't she?'

'Only because I called and asked her to come.' Okay, begged. It wasn't a moment his pride felt particularly good about. 'And like I said, she's not staying.'

He'd given her space. He'd respected her choices. And it hadn't made one bit of difference.

Leo sighed, and Seb couldn't help but feel he wasn't getting whatever point his older brother was trying to make.

'What I'm saying is…you gave me some good advice, and I'm glad I followed it. But I can't help but think you've been following your own advice a little too long.'

'Too long?' Seb frowned.

'Maria's been gone for, what? A year?' Leo asked.

'About that.' Sebastian couldn't bring himself to admit that he knew it was, in fact, twelve months and fifteen days.

'Well, waiting on love is all very well and good. But maybe sometimes love needs a bit of a push. A bit of effort.'

Love. He loved Maria—of course he did. She'd always been a part of his life, part of the family, and he loved her as much as he loved Noemi or his parents. But theirs had never been a romance as such.

Maybe that was what had been missing. Something to think about at least.

Leo cleared his throat, obviously a little uncomfortable about the very personal turn the conversation had taken. They didn't really know each other well enough to be baring their souls, Sebastian thought. He'd been astonished when Leo had called him from New York to ask what he should do about Anissa—until he'd realised that his brother simply didn't *have* anyone else to talk to about such things.

And neither, it seemed, did he. Noemi would be firmly on Maria's side, as always. His parents were gone, and his other friends, business acquaintances…he'd never even told them Maria had left in the first place. He'd had to keep up the facade of the perfect businessman and family man after all, even if everything about his life, family and business was crumbling around him. If anyone had asked, he'd just told them Maria and Frankie were visiting her parents for a few weeks. Making sure Frankie's grandparents didn't miss out on watching him grow up.

The way his own *papà* had.

'Actually, I didn't track you down out here to talk about your love life,' Leo said.

'I appreciate you not adding the word "dismal" in there,' Seb joked, making Leo smile. 'So, what did you want to talk to me about?' Whatever it was had to be better than the unending panic and echoing sorrow about the state of his family.

Leo took a long breath. Then he said, 'The business.'

CHAPTER THREE

WITH A SIGH, Noemi settled onto the bed beside her, and Maria smiled gratefully as her sister-in-law wrapped an elegant arm around her shoulder.

'So, are we finally going to talk about why you left?' Noemi asked. 'I mean, apart from the fact that my brother is an idiot.'

Maria felt a stab of guilt. It wasn't just Sebastian she'd left behind when she'd run—it had been her best friend, her whole family. She'd always felt closer to the Cattaneos than her own parents, and not having any siblings of her own, Noemi and Sebastian had filled that gap.

Yet every time Noemi had tried to talk to her about Sebastian over the last year, Maria had changed the subject. She just hadn't been ready to admit how stupid she'd been over the whole thing.

Who expected a marriage of convenience to blossom into true love, outside the movies and romance novels, anyway?

'Why do you think I left?' Maria stalled, knowing it was cowardly even as she did it.

'Why do *I* think you left? Or why does *Sebastian* think you left?' Noemi always had been too perceptive for her own good.

'Both, I guess.' Maria couldn't deny a certain curiosity as to Sebastian's reaction to her departure. And heaven knew he'd never talk to *her* about it.

When he'd found her packing, the day after that awful argument, he'd asked her to stay. And when she'd refused, told him he'd never understand, he'd stood aside and watched her go. But she knew he'd been thinking she'd come back soon enough and he just had to wait her out.

Well, he'd been wrong, hadn't he? And then he'd been too proud to ask her to come back. Until now.

Noemi tilted her head to the side as she studied her, then nodded, as if satisfied by what she saw. Maria didn't dare ask exactly what that was.

'I think he thought that you were feeling neglected,' Noemi said. 'I mean, the moment you came back from your honeymoon he threw himself into the expansion, folding your family's business into Cattaneo Jewels. Even I noticed that he was working all hours—more than he had before, ever—and that didn't change when you had Frankie.'

'No. It didn't.' The memory of those lonely days was too close to the surface for her not to feel it all over again. The aching loneliness that came from being with a baby, all day long, with no support. Seb had suggested they hire a nanny, of course, so she'd have some help—it wasn't as though they couldn't afford it. But since Seb had stopped involving her in any of his business dealings or conversations the minute she'd fallen pregnant—claiming he didn't want her suffering any stress at all—she hadn't seen the point. She loved looking after Frankie, even when it was hard and lonely.

Next, he'd suggested baby groups, which she'd tried but had never really felt she'd fitted in with. Besides, all the other mums and babies in the world had been unable to give her what she'd really wanted. Needed, even.

Sebastian's support.

Sebastian's *love*.

Unfortunately, it seemed that Sebastian was incapable of giving her that.

At least until then he'd made her feel part of his family. They'd sat up talking for hours, about the business, of course, but about so many other things, too. The world around them, places they'd like to travel to, things they'd like to do.

She'd imagined them doing them all together once they were married. But for Sebastian it seemed they were only daydreams.

'As for me...' Noemi trailed off, watching Maria with a sad look on her face. 'I didn't think you wanted to go at all.'

Far, far too perceptive.

'I didn't,' Maria admitted with a sigh. 'But at the same time… I knew I had to, and I'm glad now that I did. It was the right decision for me, and for Frankie.'

'You definitely seem more…certain, if that makes sense,' Noemi said. 'Like you know what you want your life to be now.'

'Maybe I do.' It was just a shame she couldn't see any way to make sure she got it. But even if a happy-ever-after with Sebastian was off the table, that didn't mean she couldn't have a full and happy life *without* him. 'I've been learning a lot about myself since I've been away. I mean, Seb and I got married when I was so young… I'd never really been alone before. And this time I was alone with Frankie, taking care of him every day, learning what he needed—and what I needed. It's definitely been…educational.'

And hard and lonely and difficult—but also fulfilling, rewarding and so full of love that some days Maria just cried because of how *lucky* she was, instead of for everything she'd lost.

But she didn't tell Noemi that part.

'Maybe that's what seems so different about you,' Noemi said reflectively. 'You seem *grown up*. Not that you weren't before, of course, but it's different now. Like you're the adult in the room. The mother, I suppose.'

'Not the only one for long,' Maria said, with a soft smile. 'Did I tell you how incredibly happy I am for you? And for Max, of course.'

Noemi's face lit up at the mention of her fiancé and their babies. 'You did. But I'm always happy to hear it again!'

Impulsively, Maria threw her arms around her sister-in-law's shoulders and held her tight. 'I'm *so* happy for you. You give me hope.'

'Hope?' Noemi asked, frowning as she pulled away. 'What do you mean?'

'Well, if everything can work out so perfectly for you, maybe I can still find that sort of happiness one day.'

'Just not with Sebastian?' Noemi said sadly. 'Maria… I know he's a pig-headed idiot a lot of the time, but Sebastian… He means well, I think. And this last year, without you…he's just been so *sad*. And annoying and irritable, of course, but mostly sad.'

Maria looked down at her hands. Annoyed or angry, she'd expected. She hadn't expected sad. In fact, she'd imagined he'd have been frustrated for a few days and crash around the place in a black mood, then he'd get distracted by some work crisis or another and forget he'd ever had a wife or child until it was all over.

That was what he'd done when she'd been there, after all.

'Yeah, well. I was sad when I was with him, but he didn't notice that. He didn't notice anything, really. It was as if…the moment we were married I became invisible to him. Another item ticked off his "must do before thirty" list, or something. Even Frankie… I know he loves him, but sometimes I think he sees him more as an heir than a son.'

She knew why, of course, as well as Noemi did. That was how Salvo had always treated Seb—the same way Maria's father had always treated her, as an asset, to marry off as he saw best, to further his own business endeavours. That was one of the things they'd had in common as teenagers—the knowledge that their function was more important than who they were as a person.

The only difference was that Seb's parents had adored and loved him—even as they'd pushed him to greater heights and bigger achievements. For Maria's father, marrying Seb was the best she could ever hope for—her entire self-worth wrapped up in someone else's abilities.

'Maria…you know what it was like for Seb growing up. Our parents were wonderful, loving people—especially to me. But for Seb…our father was different with him. Seb was in training from the moment he could see over the counter in Cattaneo Jewels HQ. He had so much to learn, you see, and it was so important to Papà that Seb know everything he needed to take over the business one day—'

'And then they left the controlling share to the son they'd not seen since the day he was born,' Maria finished, surprised at the anger she felt on Seb's behalf.

It seemed however hard she tried to leave her marriage behind, the emotions it brought up in her still remained.

Noemi pulled a face. 'Yeah, that's all...messy. But I'm hoping we can find a way to work it all out. I mean, we're a family, right?' The look she gave Maria made it very clear that she was including her sister-in-law in that statement.

A messed-up, separated, bizarre family with history and baggage. But a family.

'Yes, we are,' Maria agreed with a sigh. The Cattaneos had been her family long before she'd married Seb. They'd given her a place that had felt like home when her own had felt cold and empty, when her parents had gone away on trips without her, or been too busy with the business to pay her any attention. Despite Salvo's focus on training Seb, he'd always made sure they'd had time as a family, too. It was just a shame that seemed to be the one thing he *hadn't* taught his son.

Salvo and Nicole might be gone, but their children remained—and from the look in Noemi's eye, Maria knew her friend wouldn't let them all drift apart without their parents there. And because of Frankie, Maria would always be tied to them, whatever happened between her and her husband.

Noemi beamed, her radiant glow almost too bright to look at. 'I'm sorry. I just want everyone I love to be as happy as I am.'

'Trust me, I want that, too,' Maria replied. 'But right now I'd settle for just getting through this Christmas without having my heart broken.' Again.

Taking her arm, Noemi pulled Maria up from the bed. 'Come on. We're going to go downstairs and find your gorgeous little boy, pour you a glass of wine, and just enjoy all being together for Christmas. Okay?'

'Okay.' Resigned to making the most of her visit, Maria smiled and followed her sister-in-law back down the stairs.

And really, when Noemi put it like that, Christmas at the chalet sounded pretty good. She could enjoy this Christmas. Frankie could get to know his *papà* again, and maybe they could find middle ground between the past year and the one before it. One that gave them all what they needed to feel content at least, if not the incandescent happiness Noemi had found.

Maria could get back to the new life she'd forged for herself, and even if it never felt totally complete without Seb, perhaps he could still be enough a part of their lives to satisfy him and give Frankie the father he deserved.

It wouldn't be everything. But maybe it would be enough.

It would have to be.

Seb felt an icy chill that had nothing to do with the Mont Coeur snow sneak up his spine at his brother's words. 'The business?' he echoed.

This was it. This was when Leo told him that he wanted more than just a controlling share of Cattaneo Jewels—this was where his big brother took it over completely. Pushed him out and made the company his own.

And then what would he have left?

It made sense, in a way. Leo was the hotshot businessman—and he'd made it by himself. All his successes, wealth, everything were down to Leo. He hadn't had Salvo Cattaneo guiding his every move, telling him when he was about to screw up and helping him fix it. Leo hadn't had anyone. Not their parents, not his useless-sounding adoptive family. All he'd been able to rely on—and put his success down to—was his own hard work and natural talent.

Sebastian, on the other hand... His father had spent years drilling him in exactly what was expected from the heir to the family business, and

Seb had worked like hell to prove himself. But it hadn't been enough, had it? Salvo had still left the controlling share of the business to Leo, not Seb.

No wonder Leo wanted to shake things up. He'd have his own ways of doing things, new ideas and exciting possibilities.

And, sure, Seb had kept things afloat in the meantime, kept the profits ticking over nicely, thank you. But he had just been building on what was already there, not creating anything new. Even Noemi, as the face of Cattaneo Jewels, had had more influence on the shape of the company, from the outside, anyway. She'd been pushing for more, too, and as much as Seb had known she was capable of it, he'd been holding back on letting her in.

This was his responsibility, Salvo had always told him. It was up to Seb to make the company a success, to look after his sister and his mother if anything happened to him.

How badly must he have failed for things to have come to this?

But then Leo spoke again, and Seb's understanding of the world shifted once more.

'I want to sign my shares in the family business over to you.'

Seb turned to stare at his brother in astonishment. 'You're walking away? After everything, you're turning your back on your family?'

How? Leo had admitted he'd spent his whole life without a family. How could he walk away just when he'd found them? Just when Sebastian had thought they might be finding some common ground…

But Leo was smiling. Indulgently, even.

Wait. What was he missing?

Apart from the opportunity to get back what he'd always wanted—control of Cattaneo Jewels. How was it possible that he'd missed the implications of that, even for a moment? He'd been too concerned with the idea of losing his brother when he'd only just found him.

Huh. *That* was a surprise.

'I'm not walking away from our family, Seb,' Leo said. 'I'm just putting the responsibility for the business back where it belongs.'

'With…me?'

Leo nodded. 'You're the one who has worked so hard to build the business up, to keep it flourishing even when you were grieving for our parents. You're the one who deserves it.'

'But our parents… This was their dying wish.' And as much as Seb wanted to reach out and grab what Leo was offering, now he knew it didn't mean his brother leaving, and as great as it would be to take back control of his life in some small way, he knew he couldn't deny his parents' desires like that.

'I don't think it was,' Leo said, shaking his head. He sat forward, angling his body towards Seb as he spoke, and for a moment Seb could imagine that they were young boys together, plotting an adventure behind their parents' backs.

'It was in the will,' Seb said stubbornly.

'A will that was written years ago,' Leo pointed out. 'Before they ever knew if they would find me. I've been thinking about this a lot—hell, I've been thinking about a lot of things lately.'

'Ever since you met Anissa,' Seb guessed.

Leo laughed. 'Yeah, perhaps. Anyway, the point is, that will…it was a way to bring our family together if our parents weren't there to do it themselves. And it's done that, right? We're all here, at Mont Coeur, in time for Christmas.'

'I…guess so.'

'So it's done its job. I don't need those shares to remind me I'm your brother, or that Noemi is my sister. And I hope I don't need them to earn my place in this family.'

'Of course not!' However badly he might have reacted to the discovery of a secret brother, now that Leo was there, Seb would fight anyone who said he wasn't a Cattaneo or didn't belong with them.

Leo grinned. 'Then why keep them? I've got

my own businesses to run and, to be honest, you know more about the jewellery industry than I ever will. Or even want to. Jewellery isn't my thing.'

'That's true.' Seb could feel his spirits rising for the first time since he'd seen Maria standing on the doorstep and Frankie hiding his face against her coat.

'I'll speak to the lawyer tomorrow.' Getting to his feet, Leo clapped a hand on Sebastian's shoulder. 'Make it all legal as soon as the terms of the will allow me to.'

'Thanks.' Seb stared up at Leo, hoping his brother could see the sincerity in his eyes in the fading light. 'I mean it, Leo. Thank you.'

'You're welcome.' Leo started to move away towards the door of the chalet but then stopped and looked back. 'And you know, Seb, I may not have been your big brother for the last thirty-odd years. But if you need one, I'll take up the job any time you ask.'

He turned and walked away into the chalet before Seb had to come up with a response to that. Which was probably for the best, as he definitely didn't have one.

He hadn't known what to expect, meeting Leo. All he'd been told to start with was that he had a brother he'd never known existed. Then the particulars had trickled in—hotshot, self-made New

York businessman. It wasn't until he'd met Leo that he'd understood some of the other aspects of his life without his family. And not until his parents' will had been read that he'd understood what Leo had meant to them.

When his parents had died, Seb had felt like he'd lost everything. After Maria leaving, and then later with the will…everything had seemed so changed and beyond his control.

But maybe he needed to start focusing on what he had left. Counting his blessings, so to speak. A sister, who was truly blissfully happy for the first time in who knew how long, and a new brother-in-law and twin nieces or nephews to go with it. A big brother, who knew when to talk and when to walk away, who wanted to be part of the family even though he had no ties to them. A business that he could take to new heights, he knew, now he had the chance.

A son he adored with every inch of his being, even if he didn't always show it. And a chance to build the father-son relationship he'd always wanted. One that kept the best aspects of Salvo's parenting but without all the pressure, perhaps.

And Maria. The only woman he'd ever imagined marrying, spending his life with. And still the most beautiful woman he'd ever seen.

Theirs may not have been a love story—no romantic nights out, falling in love—but it was *their* story, and Seb wasn't ready for it to end. Maria was his wife, and he didn't want that to change.

So maybe he didn't have her, not any more. But he *did* have a second chance to win her back. If he could figure out how.

As Sebastian opened the front door to the chalet and stood, watching his blessings as they gathered around the huge Christmas tree, he knew he couldn't squander that chance.

Maybe his marriage had been one of convenience to start with, but did that mean he couldn't make it something more? Add a little romance, find out what Maria needed from him to be happy? If he could give it, he would, to keep one small aspect of his life in order. To stop one thing spiralling beyond his control.

But most of all to give him his son back.

Maria lifted Frankie to touch one of his parents' favourite tree ornaments, his little face lit up with a joy that was reflected in Maria's smile, and Seb felt his heart contract.

Maria seemed so much more confident, and even more content than she had before she'd left. He knew that proving to her—and maybe even to himself—that they could find that same happiness together wouldn't be easy.

But he had to try.

It was what his parents would have wanted. It was what *he* wanted, if he was honest with him-

self. Leo was right. He'd spent too long waiting for Maria to realise that she wanted to come
home. It was time to show her why she should.
To prove to her that they could be happy again.

They'd been happy once, right? He smiled as he
thought about their honeymoon. There had been
romance *then*, at least, after their vows had been
made—romantic walks on the beach, candlelit
dinners and conversation, and long, lazy love-
making at night.

That was what they needed again. What he
needed to find here at Mont Coeur to remind her
how they could be. Okay, maybe the beach was
out—but snowy walks at Christmas in the Alps?
What could be more romantic?

He could do it, he was sure. He just had to convince Maria to let him try.

'What are you doing, lurking in doorways?'
Noemi asked, as she came up behind him.
'Shouldn't you be in there with your wife and
son?'

Sebastian favoured her with a smile, realising
that Noemi was someone else he needed to make
more of an effort with. She'd be leaving with Max
soon, after all. If he wanted to repair their sibling
relationship, it had to be now—and when better
than Christmas, anyway?

But first Maria and Frankie.

'I'm going to win her back, Noemi,' he murmured, excitement jangling through his veins at the idea. 'We're going to be happy again.'

Noemi beamed, and placed a kiss against his cheek. 'Well, it's about time,' she whispered in his ear.

CHAPTER FOUR

It was so comfortable in many ways, being back in the chalet where she'd spent so many happy times before, that it came as a surprise over and over every time something jarred with her memories of the place. A reminder that she was a guest here only, or of all the things that had changed since she'd left a year ago.

They'd all enjoyed drinks and a sort of help-yourself supper, before settling down in the main living space of the chalet together. Leo and Anissa had headed back to their own chalet—apparently Leo didn't feel completely at home with them just yet, Maria thought—but Max and Noemi had joined Seb, Frankie and her for the evening. Noemi had put some soft festive music on and kept the conversation light and inconsequential.

Maria was grateful for her friend's hostess skills. She couldn't imagine how awkward the evening would have been alone with Sebastian. It was difficult enough to relax as it was.

Maria looked up at the ornaments on the tree and remembered hanging them with Nicole in years gone by, a pang of sorrow pricking her heart again as she gazed around the room and saw the empty spaces where Seb's parents would have been.

Nicole, she thought, would have been fussing around over everyone, keeping glasses topped up and the mood merry. Salvo would have been settled in his usual chair—the one that sat empty even now—by the window, watching the snow fall and enjoying the chatter of his family around him.

And, oh, they'd both have been *so happy* at Noemi's news. Not so much the princess part particularly, or the moving away to another country. But the babies and the glow of joy that had followed her around since she and Max had figured out their future together would have thrilled them. Noemi was happy, so they would have been happy.

She had no idea what they'd have made of her and Seb now. Or even what they had thought about her leaving. She suspected Seb had told them to leave her alone, probably expecting all the time that she'd change her mind and come back if they didn't nag her.

Maria remembered the day she and Seb had told his parents that they were expecting Frankie. While Maria's own father had merely nodded and said, 'Good job,' and her mother had set about organising christening dates and invitation lists to show the baby off as soon as he arrived, Nicole and Salvo had each hugged her tightly and whispered loving congratulations in her ear.

She knew that giving them an heir to Cattaneo Jewels—along with the merger with her father's business—was the reason she'd been married off to Sebastian in the first place. But the Cattaneos had never made her feel that way, even when her own family had. They'd been genuinely happy to have her as part of the family, and delighted at the news that that family would be expanding.

She'd been *wanted* here, in a way she'd never really felt wanted back home on her parents' estate. Maybe that was the real reason why she'd agreed to the marriage in the first place.

No, she couldn't lie to herself about that. It hadn't been about business or family for her.

She'd fought against it to start with. When her parents had called her home from university, sat her down and told her she wouldn't be going back, she'd thought they were joking. When they'd explained the financial predicament the business was in, she'd thought she could fix it. She, with half a business degree, had wanted to try. To help her father turn things around.

But he hadn't wanted her to.

Instead, he'd arranged a merger with his old friend Salvo Cattaneo. One that would leave him better off and able to retire. But her father

couldn't let go of Rossi Gems quite that easily—
he'd wanted a physical stake in the new company.

Her.

Her marriage to Seb would give him prestige,
give her and her children the company name, and
leave them all wealthy and happy—at least, that
had been the plan.

But even her father hadn't been able to *make*
Maria marry a man she didn't want to, not in this
day and age. And so she'd argued, she'd cried,
she'd bargained…and in the end she'd given in.
Not because it was what her parents had wanted,
or because it had made good business sense, but
because of the small voice at the back of her mind
that had told her that this was her chance. Her
shot at happiness.

Maria had agreed to marry Seb because she
was already in love with him—had been for
years, long before she'd left for university. Ever
since an icy night another Christmas, long ago, at
the Cattaneo villa near her parents' estate, when
he'd made her feel like the most important girl
in the world.

She'd hoped—naively, it seemed—that maybe
one day he could come to feel the same way about
her.

But if the other Cattaneos had welcomed her as
family, she'd known deep down she'd only ever
really been a convenience to Sebastian. He'd told

her as much that last, awful week before she'd left. He'd needed a wife to appear the respectable businessman he was so desperate to be, and he'd wanted an heir to keep the family name alive. It hadn't been the money or the business for Seb either, she was sure. Marrying her had made his father proud—and that was always what Seb had cared about most.

But now…now Salvo wasn't there to judge Sebastian's successes or failures any more. Would that change things?

Maria couldn't help but smile at the glimmer of hope that it just might. That without his father's overbearing presence Seb might finally realise that some things mattered more than the family business.

'He's almost asleep.' Seb's deep, soft voice startled her out of her reverie, and she made a small, surprised noise. Seb chuckled. How long had it been since she'd heard that sound? 'And so are you, by the sound of it.'

'I'm awake,' Maria disagreed. 'Just thinking. But you're right about Frankie.'

The two-year-old was sprawled across her lap, his eyes starting to flutter closed. As Maria watched, his eyelids would start to fall, then he'd jerk himself awake, as if unwilling to miss a moment of what was going on around him.

'He seems…happier to be here now,' Seb said tentatively.

'Max gave him ice cream and cookies,' Maria replied. 'A sure way to any boy's heart.'

Seb's answering smile didn't reach his eyes. 'When Frankie first arrived, I was a bit worried he'd forgotten all about us.'

Maria winced. She was the one who'd kept Frankie away and, however good her reasons, she couldn't avoid feeling some guilt about that. Especially when she thought about Salvo and Nicole, and how they'd missed out on watching Frankie grow the last months of their lives. Photos and video calls weren't the same.

And now it was too late.

'It's been a long year for all of us,' she said. 'And a very long day for this little boy.'

Hoisting Frankie back into a seated position, she cuddled him around his middle. Then, leaning in, she whispered against the soft hair behind his ear. 'Time for bed, *piccolo*.'

Frankie groaned his disagreement but he didn't argue very hard, which Maria knew meant he was exhausted. Shifting him in her arms, she prepared to carry him up the stairs to their room— only for Sebastian to stand first and reach down to take him.

'Can I?' he asked, and the need in his voice made Maria's heart hurt.

She could give him this much at least. 'Papà's going to carry you up to bed, Frankie. Okay?'

'Mmm…' Frankie said sleepily. 'You come, too?'

'Of course,' she promised.

They said quick goodnights to Noemi and Max, who were also heading to their rooms—although from the way they touched each other, hand on hand or elbow, Maria suspected sleep wasn't the first thing on the agenda for them—and made their way to the stairs.

She was so preoccupied with getting Frankie settled that it didn't occur to Maria until they reached the suite that once Frankie was asleep, the moment she'd been dreading would have finally arrived.

She'd be alone with her husband for the first time in a year. And she had no idea what to say to him.

Sebastian held Frankie tight against his chest as they climbed the stairs, loving every moment of having his son in his arms. The way his small body moved in and out with every breath. The softness of his hair against Seb's cheek. The tiny hand gripping his jumper. The long lashes covering hazel eyes, sooty against his skin. Seb drank in every second of the experience until it was a wrench to place him down on the small twin bed in the suite's second bedroom.

Frankie was almost asleep now, barely able to keep his eyes open. Maria undressed him, murmuring reassurance to him the whole time, then changed him into his pyjamas with a quiet efficiency Seb couldn't help but admire. She'd always been a fantastic mother, but the closeness between her and their son appeared to have only grown while they'd been away.

He just wished he'd been there to see it.

'Could you find his fox, please?' Maria asked, motioning towards the half-unpacked suitcase on the other bed. Maria's bed, he supposed, disliking the thought even as it passed through his head.

She should be with him. Not even because he wanted her physically—although of course he did, he always had—but just because he wanted to hold her in his arms while he slept, in case he woke in the night and thought her return was nothing but a dream, and needed the reassurance that she was really here, at last.

He just wanted to hold on to her. Was that so bad?

'Seb?' Maria was staring at him. Why was she staring at him? And looking meaningfully at the suitcase…?

Oh! The fox!

With a burst of speed Seb crossed the room and

started rooting through the bag for Frankie's toy fox. He'd had the stuffed animal since his birth, a gift from his grandparents, Seb's parents, and Seb was touched to discover he still slept with it, even after so long away.

His *mamma* would have liked that, Seb knew. She'd spent hours searching the toy stores for exactly the right animal for her first grandson to love.

'A first toy is important, Sebastian,' she'd told him when he'd complained. 'A first friend, a first love, a companion in this strange new world he's been thrust into. Your son has to have the right one.'

'You make it sound like a marriage, Mamma,' Seb had joked, but she'd only smiled knowingly at him.

Since she'd always known a hundred times more about the world that he ever would, he hadn't commented on it.

He missed that. Missed her. Missed being able to ask her what it was he didn't understand yet.

He held the fox against his cheek for a moment before handing it to Maria, but if she noticed, she didn't say anything.

Seb watched as Maria tucked the blanket around Frankie, even as his little hands grabbed the fox and held it under his chin, its fluffy tail brushing his cheek. For a moment he looked just like the baby Seb remembered. Like no time had passed at all.

He pressed a kiss to his son's forehead and whispered, 'Sweet dreams, *piccolo*,' just like he had every night before he'd gone to bed when Frankie had lived with him.

Then he stepped back and saw Maria's wary face, her shorter hair, her harder eyes, and knew that everything *had* changed.

And it was his job to change things back again.

Romance. That was his way in, he was almost sure. Maria had felt neglected before she'd left— had thrown it in his face when they'd argued the night before she'd packed her bags and walked out.

'You don't even see me!' she'd yelled. 'Sometimes I'm not sure you'd even notice if I left.'

But he'd noticed. Boy, how he'd noticed.

Seb may not have his mother there to set him right, but he knew exactly what she'd have said. *Take care of your wife, Sebastian. Look after your family.*

And so that was what he was going to do. Starting with talking to Maria. Listening to Maria. Letting her know how much he wanted her there, and how far he was willing to go to keep her with him.

Whatever it took.

'How about a drink by the fire?' he suggested,

softly, so as not to disturb Frankie. Maria looked up at him in surprise. 'I think we've got a lot to talk about. Don't you?'

She should have thought about this more—about what she'd say once she was alone with Sebastian again. And she had, to a point. She'd been imagining this conversation for a year—ever since she'd left.

But she realised now, too late, that in her head the conversation was always Seb talking, and her unable to get a word in edgeways as he listed her faults and derided her for breaking her marriage vows. Told her what a terrible wife and mother she was. How disappointed in her he was. How he'd married her for only one reason, and she hadn't lived up to her side of the bargain.

Just like her father had done when she'd arrived home with Frankie.

She hadn't ever imagined they'd be sitting together on the squashy, cosy sofa in their old suite, drinking good red wine in front of the fire, waiting for each other to start.

Maria had never been much good at silence. She was always going to crack first.

'Look, I know we have a lot to talk about. And that you must have questions. And… I don't blame you for being angry with me—'

'I never said I was angry with you,' Seb said, so calmly she couldn't help but believe him.

'You're…not?' she asked, just to check.

'I was,' Seb admitted. 'When you first left… just ask Noemi. I was like a bear with a sore head for months.'

'She might have mentioned that.' Only with slightly less polite words when it came down to it.

'But looking at you now…' Seb shook his head, a slight smile on his lips. 'I may not have liked it, but I can see why you had to go.'

Maria blinked at him. Did he really know? Did he, at last, understand why she'd been unable to stay, been unable to see him smile at her while looking through her every day? Did he realise how much it had hurt to be so close to him and yet feel so much difference between them?

No. Apparently not.

'I mean, you seem so much more content now. Like you've found yourself, I guess,' Seb went on, oblivious to how her heart was cracking. 'I get that I didn't give you the attention you needed, that I worked too much, that you were alone with Frankie a lot of the time.'

'That was part of it,' Maria said cautiously. But Seb didn't hear her caution, it seemed. The same way he hadn't heard her words the night before she'd left.

'This isn't enough for me, Seb. And I realise

now you can't give me what I need. You're not capable of it.'

Not capable of love. Or not capable of loving *her*. Either way, it added up to the same thing, really.

'The thing is, I realised something today,' Seb went on. 'I don't want to be an absentee father or even a detached husband. I don't want to spend my life without you or without Frankie.' He took a deep breath, and Maria couldn't help but admire the way his broad chest moved, how handsome his profile was in the firelight.

Oh, God, was there really *no* hope for her?

'I want us to use this time, while we're all here together over Christmas, to find a better way forward,' Seb said. 'One that gives you what you need but doesn't cut me out of your lives so completely. A way for us to work together, to make our marriage what we always promised it would be. A partnership.'

Maria met his gaze, and saw the sincerity there. He wanted this for real—wanted *her*, even.

Just not the way she'd always dreamed of.

He wanted his family back together—and wasn't that only natural after losing his parents, and all the other changes he'd been through recently? She was familiar, easy. And, yes, of course he loved Frankie.

But none of that was the same as loving her.

'What do you say?' Seb shifted closer on the sofa, angling his body into her. They were so close she could smell the familiar scent of his skin, could reach out and touch his hair—kiss him, even. And it would be so, so easy to fall back into those old patterns. To let him hold her and to feel safe in his arms. To remember how they used to move together, and how incredible it had felt.

To let herself love him with her whole heart again, only to have it break even harder this time when he still couldn't love her the way she needed.

Pulling back, Maria shook her head. 'Seb, I'm not here to stay. You know that. Frankie and I… We only came for Christmas.'

'I know, I know.' Seb flashed her a devastating smile. 'But can you blame me for wanting more?'

'No, but… I have a life somewhere else now. And so does Frankie.'

Admittedly, her life mostly revolved around Frankie, and her part-time business degree. Thankfully her mother, while endlessly disappointed in her, didn't take out that disappointment on Frankie, who spent many happy days with his grandmother while his mother studied. If nothing else good had come out of this year, that at least was more than she'd truly hoped for when she'd left. And even if her relationship with her father was ruined for good after the last few months, in some ways that was a relief, too. She didn't have to try to be the Maria he wanted any more either. She could just be herself.

'Is there…? Have you met someone else?' What was it she heard in Seb's voice as he asked that? It sounded like…like fear, perhaps. But why on earth would Seb be afraid of that? Unless it was his ongoing terror of not appearing to have the perfect life.

The thing Maria had never been able to understand was that Seb was gorgeous, rich, funny when he wanted to be, and generally a good guy. He could have had women lining up down the street for him, especially since she'd left.

But Noemi had said he'd stayed completely alone. The only reason Maria could think of for that was that the business and his reputation were still more important to him than his own happiness—never mind hers or anyone else's.

That was what had convinced her, finally, that she'd made the right decision in leaving.

But she'd never been able to take that next step herself. 'No,' she said, looking down at her hands as she shook her head slightly. 'I mean, a couple of times people tried to set me up on blind dates and stuff, but no. There's no one else.'

'Good. That's…that means there's still hope.'

'Hope?' Maria looked up into his eyes and saw something else there now. The same sort of determination she was more used to seeing when he was undertaking a difficult new business deal. Or once, just after they'd married, when he'd set about finding out everything she liked and loved between the sheets.

A determined Seb could accomplish great things. Her body remembered. Vividly.

'Hope that I can fix this. If you'll let me try.'

God, she'd never been able to resist him when he looked like that. Not when he focused all his attention on her so completely, determined to do whatever it took to please her.

If only he'd looked like that more often, she'd probably never have left.

'Okay,' she said, the word coming out raspy. She took a sip of wine to soothe her throat and her nerves. It was only until Christmas. On Boxing Day she and Frankie would leave, unless something fundamental shifted in her relationship with Seb. She could give him until Christmas, couldn't she? Call it his Christmas present. 'We can try.'

CHAPTER FIVE

SEBASTIAN WAS UP early the next morning—not for work reasons for once but because he was eager to start a new, even more important project.

Project Win Back Wife and Child.

Maybe it needed a better name than that, he mused as he stepped into the shower, hoping the warm water would wake him up a bit. He hadn't slept as well as he normally did. For some reason, after a year of getting used to not having Maria in his bed beside him, last night had thrown him straight back to those first, lonely days after she'd left. Rather than sprawling across the bed as he'd taken to doing over the last twelve months to make it feel less empty, he'd spent the night hours reaching for someone who hadn't been there, and waking himself up when he'd realised he'd been alone.

Clearly, he needed this project more than ever.

Maybe Project Family was the name he was looking for. He had a feeling that Noemi would approve.

He hoped so, anyway, because he was going to need her help to pull it off.

By the time Seb was showered and dressed, there was still no sign of the door to Maria and

Frankie's room opening. He loitered outside for a few moments, listening, but all was quiet.

Deciding to let them sleep in, Seb headed downstairs to find his sister.

Noemi was, as he'd expected, brewing coffee in the kitchen—decaf, in her case, it seemed, but fortunately she had some full-strength stuff on the go, too.

'Can I steal a cup of that?' he asked, settling himself on one of the counter stools to watch her work. Now he knew about her pregnancy, it was impossible to miss the slight curve of her usually slender body, or the way her clothes skimmed over it. Not to mention the glow of happiness that surrounded her.

'I was making it for Max.' She scowled at him, rather ruining the pregnancy goddess image.

'Please? I assure you, my need is greater. I need energy for my plans today.' He was wheedling, he knew, but Noemi was a soft touch sometimes, so if it worked it was worth it.

'Plans?' She poured a cup of the coffee and pushed it towards him, one eyebrow elegantly arched. 'Are these Maria plans?'

Seb nodded, taking a sip of the steaming hot drink. 'That's the idea.'

Noemi leaned forward against the counter between them, her elbows on the wooden surface. 'Then how can I help?'

Seb grinned. 'I was hoping you would ask that.'

'Because you have no idea how to win a woman over?' Noemi asked.

'Hey! She married me in the first place, didn't she?' Seb pointed out.

Noemi rolled her eyes. 'That was a business deal. No one ever denied that you were good at those.'

Well, it was the closest thing to a compliment that he was likely to get from his sister these days, so Seb decided to take it.

'It wasn't just business,' he argued, almost for the sake of it. Everyone knew that if it hadn't been for Maria's father's business troubles, she never would have married him. And he'd probably never have got around to getting married at all, too busy with the company. But business wasn't all there had ever been between them—especially after the vows had been made and he'd discovered how much he adored making love to his wife... But that wasn't the point. 'We were friends. Partners, even. And we're parents. That doesn't count for nothing, you know.'

'Hey, I'm all for you two crazy kids working things out between you,' Noemi said, lifting her coffee cup in a mock toast. 'I just think you need to figure out exactly why she left, and how you can stop screwing up so badly.'

'I'm way ahead of you.' Seb tried not to sound

too smug. 'And I've always known why she left—she told me as much when we argued the night before.'

'And you listened?' Noemi asked, sounding amazed.

Seb ignored her. 'She felt ignored. Neglected. She said I didn't see her.'

'Right,' Noemi said slowly, as if there needed to be more.

'So I'm going to prove to her that I *do* see her. That if she comes home I won't ignore her. That there can be romance and that stuff in our marriage, even if it's not *why* we married.'

'"Romance and that stuff",' Noemi echoed, faintly. 'Right.'

'See! It's all going to be great.' Seb felt a lot better about his plan, having talked it through. All he needed to do was show Maria how much he wanted her there. Which was easy, because it was the truth.

'So what do you need me to do?' Noemi asked, sounding far too sceptical about the whole thing for Seb's liking. Still, he'd show her. He just needed the time to do it—and he only had until Christmas. Which meant pulling out the romance big guns from the off.

'Could you and Max watch Frankie for me today? As much as I want to spend time with the little guy, I figure that romancing Maria comes first.' After all, if that part of the plan worked, then Frankie would be around for him to spend time with every day. If it didn't…

Well. He just wasn't going to think about that. 'Will you do it?'

'Of course,' Noemi said automatically. 'But what are you and Maria going to be doing?'

Seb grinned broadly. 'We're going on a date.'

'I'm so sorry—we slept in!' Maria bustled into the kitchen, Frankie holding her hand, to find Sebastian and Noemi sipping coffee together at the counter. 'I guess we must have been more tired than I thought after travelling yesterday.' At least, Maria assumed that was why Frankie—who was always an early-morning kid—had slept in way past his normal wake-up time. Travelling and a late night, plus lots of new people, had had him zonked out for twelve straight hours.

She, on the other hand, had spent most of the night listening to Frankie breathing and thinking about her husband in the next room, and what she'd agreed to. She'd finally passed out around three in the morning, and had apparently made up for the lack of rest by oversleeping until closer to lunch than breakfast.

Frankie, dressed in his warmest clothes, bounced on his toes beside her, still excited by being at the chalet. He'd woken up perfectly rested and had bounded onto her bed to wake her up, too, keen to start his day in the snow.

'Don't worry! You haven't missed anything yet,' Noemi said, beaming.

'In fact, we were just discussing plans for the day,' Seb added. Maria couldn't help but notice that Sebastian, at least, looked relaxed, happy and as gorgeous as ever. While she felt like a nervous wreck. How was that fair?

At least she'd have Frankie as a buffer between them today. Seb couldn't possibly want to continue last night's conversation with their son around. So all she needed to do was keep things friendly and polite—and not let him get under her skin again like last night.

Easy. Right?

But then Noemi crouched down in front of Frankie, a mischievous grin on her face. 'How would you like to spend the day with Aunt Noemi and Uncle Max, munchkin?'

Maria's gaze flew to Sebastian's face, but he was smiling serenely. This was *his* plan, then. He wanted to get her alone.

Damn him.

'Noemi, you really don't have to—'

'I'd love to!' Noemi broke in. 'And so would Max. Or he will when I tell him. I mean, it's great practice for us both.'

'Right. I know. It's just... I'm not sure that

Frankie is—' Maria started again, trying to find a good enough excuse that wouldn't offend Noemi, but this time Frankie interrupted her.

'We have ice cream?' he asked, in his sweet, high voice.

Subzero temperatures and her son wanted ice cream. Naturally.

'Of course we'll have ice cream!' Noemi said gleefully. She took his hand and led him away. 'But probably not for breakfast. How about we have some pastries first, then we can go and find Uncle Max and decide what else we want to do today.'

'Okay.' Frankie sounded cheerful enough, but Maria was pretty sure he hadn't heard past 'pastries'. He loved pastries almost as much as ice cream, and at two years old he didn't have much of a handle on time just yet.

But he was happy. So she had no reason to stop him spending time with Noemi and Max. And no excuse not to spend time with Sebastian, except for the fact that she was scared of losing all the ground she'd made while she'd been away. She could feel her resistance ebbing away.

'So…lunch?' Seb asked, and Maria couldn't seem to stop herself nodding.

Ninety minutes later—after giving Noemi and Max comprehensive toddler care instructions, and explaining in great detail to Frankie the behaviour she expected from him, while knowing that despite his nodding and innocent wide eyes he wasn't going to remember any of it, then changing into something smart enough for going out and being seen around Mont Coeur with Sebastian but warm enough that she wouldn't freeze the moment she stepped outside the chalet—Seb and Maria went for lunch.

'Honestly, I'd be fine with just a burger or something,' Maria protested, as he led her towards the fanciest restaurant in Mont Coeur.

Seb gave her an amused look, as if he could tell just by looking at her that she was trying to find ways to keep this lunch short and, well, just short, really. He probably could, too. He'd always been good at reading her. On the surface, anyway. Just not when it came to the things that really mattered.

'Do you realise,' Seb said, holding open the glass door to the restaurant for her, 'this is our first ever proper date?'

'This is a date now?' Maria's eyes widened. Yeah, she really should have found a way to go snowman building with Frankie and Max.

'You, me, the best and most romantic restaurant in town… Yes, Maria, this is a date.' Seb rolled his eyes, as if waiting for her to catch up with the agenda for the day. Which she was suddenly rather afraid she had.

Seb was planning on wooing her. Romancing her. Except she knew for a fact that her husband had no experience or idea of what that should entail.

She'd known Seb since they had both been in nappies, their fathers long-time friends, neighbours and business acquaintances, with Rossi Gems providing many of the precious stones used in the Cattaneo Jewels designs. The families had grown closer as the kids had grown up together, and Maria had watched Seb change from a serious, wide-eyed boy to a gawky teenager, until he'd suddenly come into his height and build around the age of seventeen.

She'd been fifteen at the time, and definitely hadn't missed the changes in him.

When he'd left for university he'd been handsome, confident and ready to take on the business world. But he'd always been far too caught up in making his father proud to waste time on girls. Oh, she was sure he'd dated a little—and she was certain he must have had *some* experience before their wedding night, or it couldn't have been as fantastic as it had been. But women hadn't mattered to him, not the way the business did, and they'd been married less than a year after he'd finished his MBA, so it wasn't like he'd had a lot of time to play around. Besides, the idea of him taking time out from his studies to plan a dream date was sort of ridiculous.

Although a romantic restaurant was a pretty good start, she supposed. Clichéd and obvious, but at least not awful. It could have been a lot worse.

'Right.' Well, at least she knew what she was up against. Seb on a charm offensive could be quite something to watch, but she was prepared now. She could hold her own.

She frowned. Sure, she'd buy Seb not dating around much before they'd married. But… 'Wait. We *must* have gone on a date before. We've been married for years, for heaven's sake.'

'Name one,' Seb challenged.

And, of course, she couldn't. Because romance wasn't what their marriage had been about. They'd gone out, of course, but for business dinners or corporate trips or what have you. Never just to spend time in the pleasure of each other's company.

Fortunately, Maria was saved from answering by the arrival of the maître d', looking horrified that he'd missed their arrival by all of thirty seconds. He led them straight to their table, gushing over having Mr Cattaneo gracing his restaurant— and on a weekday, too!

Seb mostly ignored him, taking the offered menu and sitting down to study it as the maître d' pulled Maria's chair out for her. Copying Seb, she reached for her own menu as Seb ordered a carafe of white wine to start.

'So?' Seb peered at her over the top of his menu. 'Thought of one yet? A date, I mean.'

'What about the night we went to the theatre to see that play you were so keen on?' Maria asked. 'Doesn't that count?' Admittedly, Seb had only seen the first half because an emergency call from the office in the interval had meant he'd spent the rest of the evening on the phone in the theatre foyer, but still…

Seb put down his menu. 'I think we need to re-evaluate your criteria for a date,' he said. 'I take full responsibility—I clearly haven't been keeping up my end of the husband bargain when it comes to taking you out.'

'So, what constitutes a date by your definition?' Maria asked. Maybe there was wriggle room with one of the corporate trips…

'You and me alone—no family or business acquaintances along. Somewhere romantic, and only focused on each other.'

Huh. Well, they definitely hadn't done that—at least not since their honeymoon. And she had to admit that it didn't sound so bad. Especially if, for the first time she could remember, Seb kept his word and left work at the office. To be fair to him, he hadn't mentioned the business once since they'd left the chalet. Even now, he was smiling pleasantly at the wine waiter and tasting the white wine he'd brought them. When he nodded, the waiter poured them each a full glass.

'In that case, I agree—this might actually be our first real date since our honeymoon.' And they hadn't had any before because they hadn't needed to. The engagement had been arranged by their fathers. They'd known each other since they were children. Why would they have needed to date?

Although… Maria's mind drifted back to when she'd been fifteen, and the memory of a frosty night on a frozen lake, and Seb's hand in hers. Maybe that was the closest they'd got, and she knew for a fact that Seb wouldn't count it. He hadn't thought of her that way, even then.

But maybe now he could.

Maria lifted her glass to Seb, and he followed suit, clinking it gently against hers.

'To romance,' he said, and smiled the smile that had always made her heart flutter most.

'To romance,' she echoed.

Oh, yeah. She was in for it now.

The restaurant was everything Noemi had promised it would be when he'd asked for recommendations. The food was exquisite, the staff attentive but unobtrusive, and the atmosphere wonderfully romantic—especially with the still falling snow outside those huge glass windows.

The perfect place for his first date with his wife.

Seb watched her across the table as she delicately finished her chocolate mousse. He still wasn't used to all the changes in her.

Her hair, chopped back from halfway down her back to just above her shoulders, looked strangely more grown up somehow, although still as dark and glossy as ever. Her bright blue eyes sparkled as they always had, but there was something wary in them, as if she was holding back. She'd lost a little weight, he thought. It made her more delicate almost, except that there was nothing fragile about the woman sitting across from him.

Her dark red knitted dress clung to her slender curves, reminding him of everything he knew lay underneath it, and he ached to learn her anew that way.

She was stronger now, he was sure. He felt it somewhere inside.

It only made him want her more.

They'd talked all through lunch—mostly about Frankie and his funny toddler ways, or about their families. He'd told her a little about Leo and their growing relationship as brothers—although not about the offer of his shares, not yet. Maria, in turn, had given him a dry account of how her parents had responded to her showing up on their doorstep with Frankie in tow.

Seb knew his in-laws. He didn't need the details to imagine the scenes.

'What about you?' he asked, as Maria put down her cutlery. 'You've told me about everyone else. But what have *you* been up to over the last twelve months?'

She looked surprised that he'd asked. Had he really been that inattentive before she'd left? Probably. He had just been so used to Maria always being there, being part of his life, he'd taken her for granted. Had skimped on the romance and attention she'd deserved.

He wouldn't make that mistake again, if she gave him the chance.

'Mostly looking after Frankie,' Maria said. 'Placating my father, that sort of thing.'

Seb waited. That couldn't be all of it. He *knew* Maria.

'And... I've been taking a course. A business course.'

'Really?' Now, that *was* interesting. 'Why?'

He knew the question was a mistake the moment he asked it—the scowl on Maria's face only confirmed it for him.

'Because I should be happy to be a wife and a mother, right? Just stay home and look pretty, rather than getting my hands dirty in business?' she snapped.

'No!' Seb's eyes widened, and he put up his hands in a mock surrender. 'That's not... I only meant that you were always such a natural at business. You understood everything I ever spoke to you about, and you gave great advice. I just wondered why you felt you needed to study it again after, well...' After she'd given it up to marry him, at her father's request. *Tactful, Seb.*

But Maria's expression softened a tiny bit anyway. 'I'm sorry. I should know better. I just... I've been spending a lot of time with my father lately.'

'Ah.' Maria's father had never wanted her involved in the family business. As far as he was concerned, her only job had been to marry well enough to bring in a *man* to deal with it—as shown by his actions when he'd run his own company into the ground, then married Maria off to fix it.

Seb knew his father would have undertaken the merger without the marriage, to help his friend. But old man Rossi had just had to have a physical marker, keeping his hand in the business, and Salvo had been happy to see his son settled so easily.

Sebastian had never had much respect for his father-in-law.

'Yeah. He didn't like me taking the course much.' She looked up and met his gaze, and Seb listened carefully, knowing whatever she had to say next mattered. A lot. 'But I wanted to finish what I started, all those years ago. I'm a grown woman now. I make my own choices.'

'I never thought you weren't,' Seb said carefully. 'And I would never want to make choices for you.'

He'd just really like it if she made the ones he wanted her to make. Did that make him as bad as her father? He wasn't really sure any more.

'Good. I just wondered because…' She trailed off, leaving Seb to imagine what she might have been about to say.

Except he needed to know. He needed to know everything he'd done wrong so he could fix them. Otherwise in a matter of days she'd be walking away from him again—for good this time.

'Because?' he prompted.

'Back before we were married—and even after for a while, I suppose—you used to talk to me about the business. Ask my advice, let me help you work out the best way forward for Cattaneo Jewels. And I liked that. It was something we had in common, to connect us. My father, he never wanted me anywhere near the business end of things, but you did. You made me feel like you valued my opinions.'

'I did,' Seb said, quickly. 'Very much. You always knew the right questions to ask to help me work through things. You helped me get to the heart of whatever the problem was so I could figure out what really mattered.' His dad had been giving him more and more control and responsibility, he remembered, setting him up to take things over when he was ready to retire. Having Maria to talk things through with had made that less scary.

Had made him feel less alone.

'Then why did you stop?' Maria asked. 'The minute I got pregnant with Frankie, it was as if that was my only responsibility, the only thing I was good for any more. Giving you an heir.'

Seb's eyes widened. 'That wasn't… No, absolutely not. That wasn't what I was thinking at all.' What the hell *had* he been thinking? Everything had been so confused and frantic since then it was hard to remember. But he knew he had to.

'Then explain it to me.' Maria sat back in her seat and waited.

'I'll… I'll try.' Seb saw a waiter hovering, waiting to see if they wanted more drinks or whatever. 'Just…let me get the bill. I want to have this conversation properly, not here.'

He handed his card over to the loitering waiter, tipping generously as he paid, his mind still on the past—and its power over the present. So much of their history was tangled up in their fathers' actions. Could they unwind all of that to find a new path, a new future together?

This conversation could make or break his marriage, he was almost certain. He *had* to get it right.

Besides which, he wasn't ready for this date to be over yet. For the first time ever, he and Maria were being totally honest with each other. He didn't want to call a close to that—not before he had a chance to tackle the issues that really mattered between them.

Then he looked out of the window and saw the perfect way to keep their bubble of privacy and truthfulness.

Smiling, he replaced his card in his wallet and put it back in his jacket pocket.

'Come on,' he said, reaching for Maria's hand. 'I've got an idea.'

CHAPTER SIX

ONLY SEBASTIAN WOULD think that a romantic sleigh ride was the perfect place for the most important conversation she'd ever had in her marriage. Possibly in her life. He really was going all out with the romance thing, given his total lack of prior experience.

Although, she had to admit, it did at least give them privacy.

Up ahead, the two bright white horses clip-clopped through the streets of Mont Coeur, out towards the snowy fields and hills beyond, tugging their festive green sleigh behind them. Their driver wore thick earmuffs and had barely even grunted a welcome as Sebastian had helped her on board, so Maria was fairly sure he wasn't eavesdropping on their marital woes.

Still, they kept the conversation light to start with, each pointing out sights and sounds around them.

'Look! Ice skaters.' Seb pointed towards a frozen lake just beyond the village. 'Do you remember that night we crept out to go ice-skating on the lake at your parents' house?'

'Of course.' Maria smiled, a little wistfully. How

could she forget the night she'd fallen in love with her husband? Even if she'd never told him.

Seb's smile was more rueful. 'I probably should have been locked up for taking you out there. It was stupidly dangerous, and you were only, what, thirteen?'

'Fifteen,' Maria corrected him. 'And I wanted to go.'

'That's why I took you,' Seb said, with a grin.

Maria looked away, settling back against the padded seat, the memory flooding back. It had been the Christmas holidays, the year before Seb had left for university. The year she'd looked at him and seen a man almost—and a gorgeous one at that. Seb and Noemi had been visiting for a weekend while their parents were away. Maria had been begging her parents all day to let them skate on the frozen lake on the estate, but they'd refused to budge. Too dangerous. Too risky.

But that was what Maria had wanted. A little risk, a little danger. Anything to make her feel less trapped in her parents' house.

That night, after everyone had gone to bed, Seb had knocked on her door, a pair of ice skates dangling from his fingers.

She'd never felt more alive than she had that night, skating in the darkness with Sebastian Cattaneo. And she'd known then she'd never love anyone else either.

But she couldn't think about that now. Not when there was so much still unsettled between them.

Dragging her attention back to the present, she made herself feel the sleigh beneath her, the icy air against her skin. She wasn't fifteen any more. She had to remember that.

'I've never been on one of these before,' she admitted, watching as the snow-capped trees flew past alongside them. 'Frankie would love it. Or be terrified. No real way of telling with toddlers.'

'We'll bring him into town to see the horses, then,' Seb said. 'See how he reacts.'

We. Together. As a family. She knew that was what Seb was getting at, what he was striving for. But she needed her answers first.

Shifting in her seat, she angled her body towards him, her gloved hands resting on her lap. He looked so gorgeous in the bright, reflected light of the sun on the snow, his close-cropped dark hair showing off his strong jaw and handsome features. His green eyes looked thoughtful, as he stared out over the view of the Alps. Was he thinking about his answer? Or a work problem?

Probably the latter, since it was Seb.

'So. Have you thought of a reason yet?' she asked, not hiding the slight edge in her voice as she almost echoed his question from lunch. This was important to her. If they really wanted to repair their relationship—even if only so they could

parent Frankie more amicably long distance—
then she needed to understand what had changed
for him. Why he'd started cutting her out just
when she'd hoped they'd be growing closer.

'It's not so much thinking of a reason.' Seb gave
her a small, apologetic smile. 'It's remembering
exactly what I was thinking and feeling. I tend to
act more on instinct and logic with these things,
rather than thinking them through sometimes.'

She knew that. She knew him. Which meant
she also knew that if he could avoid thinking
about emotions and such completely and swap
them for spreadsheets and profit-and-loss statements instead, he would.

But she wasn't going to let him get away with
that today.

'I think… You remember how ill you were at
the start of your pregnancy?' he asked.

Urgh. As if she could forget. She'd thrown up
for twelve weeks straight, every day at eleven
and four like clockwork. And in between she'd
nursed a bottle of chilled water and a packet of
plain crackers. It was *not* a time she remembered
with fondness, even if it had been worth it to have
Frankie.

'Of course I remember.'

'I'd never… I'd never seen you like that before. You'd never had more than a head cold the
whole time I'd known you. Even when the rest of

us came down with chickenpox that year when I was about ten, you stayed immune.'

'I'd already had it as a toddler,' Maria recalled. 'So I was free to just laugh at your and Noemi's spots.'

'Yeah, well. Seeing you like that—sick and weak and emotional—it was kind of scary, I guess. I hated that it was my fault you felt that way, and hated even more that there was nothing I could do to make you feel better.'

Maria looked at him curiously. 'It was just pregnancy sickness, Seb. Millions of women go through it every day—many of them a lot worse than I did.'

'I know. But none of those other millions of women were my wife.'

She couldn't help herself. She reached over and took his gloved hand in hers, holding it on her lap. 'So that's why you stopped involving me in the business? Because I was getting sick?'

'Partly,' Seb said, and sighed. 'I suppose I felt like I had to make it up to you. I mean, of course I wasn't going to bother you with work stuff when you were feeling so lousy. But afterwards… I just wanted you to enjoy the pregnancy and then having Frankie. I didn't want to bother you with the business or my worries.'

'But you're my husband, Seb. Your worries should have been our worries.' That was what he'd never understood. She wanted a partnership. He wanted a wife and heir to trot out at business social events. 'And it's not like becoming a mother rotted my brain. I was still the same person I'd always been—I still cared about the business, too.'

'I know that *now*,' Seb replied. 'But back then… it felt like Frankie was your whole world, and my job was just to make sure that you and he were safe and secure and wanted for nothing—like my *papà* had always done for my mother.'

I wanted my husband, Maria thought. *I wanted your love.* But she didn't say it. However cosy this romantic sleigh ride might be, she wasn't ready to admit that yet. That she wanted them to be a team, a partnership—sure, that was what they'd promised each other, privately, when they'd agreed to their fathers' plans for their marriage.

They'd never promised love, not really.

Yes, there were those pesky wedding vows—to love, honour and cherish. But that was just something they'd had to say. Besides, there were many kinds of love. And she'd never doubted that Seb loved her as an old treasured family friend. One with whom he shared a fantastic sexual chemistry, but that was just sex. She'd had his affection, his friendship, his passion, and even his son.

She'd always known it hadn't gone any deeper. He hadn't loved her with his whole heart, in that aching, all-consuming way she'd loved him.

If he had, he could never have let her leave at all.

'I just wanted what we always promised each other,' she said instead. 'I wanted us to be a team. I wanted to feel part of it all.'

All those lonely days with Frankie and then nothing to talk about when Seb came home at night except how long the baby had napped, or how much milk he'd taken. Nothing in her life beyond nappies and sleepsuits.

She'd loved her baby, loved being a mother. But she'd longed for something more, too.

'I didn't realise.' Seb shook his head a little sadly. 'I thought... I thought you wanted the sort of marriage my parents had—your parents, too, I suppose.'

Maria laughed, a little bitterly, thinking of her parents' silent, grudging marriage. 'Trust me. That was the last thing I wanted.'

Seb squeezed Maria's hand tightly through two pairs of gloves. 'I'm sorry.' He'd been an idiot as usual. Maria hadn't just felt neglected; she'd felt sidelined. Like her opinion hadn't mattered.

He'd known well enough from his earliest days in the business, trying to earn his right to be there beyond just being the son and heir, how painful that could be. Every time he'd heard someone whisper behind his back that he wouldn't have a job if he wasn't Salvo's son, or caught a comment about nepotism, he'd doubted himself over again. He'd earned the right to be there in the end, but it had taken time.

Something he didn't have with Maria.

Okay. So he couldn't fix the past. But he could try to change the future. And if all she wanted was for them to be a partnership again, he could give her that.

'I wish I'd known how you felt,' he said. 'But now that I do…we can fix this, right? If you want more of a say in the business, that's easy. I'd love to have your help and advice again.'

She'd never believe him if he told her how much he'd missed that. Even when she'd still been there, when Frankie had been a baby. Of course, she'd been busy looking after him and, quite rightly, Frankie had been her number one concern. But he'd also missed the days when they'd used to talk. About the business, yes, but about other things, too. The future. Their hopes and dreams.

He remembered his parents doing that. While Salvo had been very much the businessman, and Nicole had been content merely to *wear* the jewellery he'd sold, rather than be involved in the company, that hadn't been the case at home at all. There they had been a partnership in the truest sense of the word. They had each had their own responsibilities, but they had always worked towards a common goal—keeping their family happy, healthy and together.

He'd lost sight of that goal with Maria, he realised suddenly. She was right. Somewhere along the way they'd stopped being a team. And he wanted more than anything to get that feeling back again.

'That would be good,' Maria said, and Seb would have celebrated—except for the cautious tone in her voice that gave him pause.

'But?'

Maria sighed, turning away to look out at the snow. For a long moment all Seb could hear was the soft fall of horse hooves on newly fallen snow and the crack in the air that told him more snow would be falling soon.

And his own internal monologue, of course, coming up with increasingly awful things that Maria might say next.

But this marriage isn't enough for me.

But you're not good enough for me.

But I want to be free to find someone who can give me what I need.

But Frankie needs a better father than you.

Finally, she looked at him again and spoke over his own dark thoughts. 'But the business has always been the easy part for you.'

Seb scoffed. 'Tell that to my shareholders.'

'You know what I mean.' She pulled her hand away from his. 'Work was always what you ran to when things were difficult. Remember how many hours you put in when I was pregnant?'

'Yeah, but that was because we were in the middle of launching the new range and starting on the expansion—'

'And what does it tell you that you can remember exactly what was happening at the office at that time, but it took you twenty minutes to remember how you were feeling, or what was going on in our marriage back then?'

Seb felt heat rushing to his face, despite the chilly air. Of course he could. He could remember every milestone on his journey through the family business—from the first day that his father had taken him to the office and told him that one day he'd be in charge, through his first internship, learning the ropes, right up to the day his father had signed over a portion of the company into Seb's name and told him he was responsible now.

Cattaneo Jewels had been a part of his life since he hadn't been much older than Frankie was now. He'd grown up knowing that the company was more than his destiny or even his birthright—it was his responsibility. His burden and his joy.

If he screwed up, it wasn't just him who lost money. It was his investors, his shareholders, his board. His staff whose jobs would be on the line. His suppliers who could go out of business. His clients who would be let down.

His father, who would be disappointed in him.

Even now Salvo was gone, Seb knew that his dad's disappointment could transcend the grave. If Seb ran Cattaneo Jewels into the ground, Salvo might actually rise up to berate him for it.

But how could he explain all that to Maria?

'I guess… I know what I'm doing with the business—at least I should do by now. And it's easy to measure success or failure. It's all there in the quarterly reports. But with relationships… it's harder somehow.'

'You need a quarterly report on our marriage? Our family?' Maria arched her dark eyebrows over her sparkling blue eyes.

'Honestly? It would probably help.' Seb sighed, slumping down a little on the bench seat of the sleigh. He hadn't just lost sight of his family goal. He'd never even set it to begin with. 'Nobody ever taught me this stuff, Maria. I was just expected to *know* how to be a husband, a father. And I… I don't.'

The admission hurt. His whole life he'd tried to be ahead of the game, to make his father proud by never messing up, by pretending he already knew everything Salvo was trying to teach him. By studying harder than everyone else, striving for the right experience, the right opportunities. Knowing the answer to every question before it was even asked.

But now…if the only way to win Maria back was by admitting he was clueless?

Then he'd do it. He'd tell her exactly how little he knew—and how much he wanted to learn.

He'd tell her everything.

Did he think she'd been taken aside as a teenager and given special wife lessons? Instruction in being a great mother, beyond the basic antenatal classes? Hints and tips on how to cuddle a toddler, or how to buck up a husband who'd had a bad day at work, or how to chase away the constant fear that something would happen to one of them?

'Nobody does, Seb,' she said, softly. 'Nobody is born knowing how to…connect to other people. It's something we all have to learn.'

'*You* know.'

Did she? She'd always assumed that what she knew about loving families came mostly from hanging out with the Cattaneos practically since birth. Her father certainly hadn't given her many clues, and her mother…her mother was the perfect, doting wife, who believed whatever her husband said was law.

Come to think of it, her mother might actually be just as disappointed in Maria as her father was after the collapse of her marriage, only she was too polite to make a scene about it. Marguerite Rossi *never* made a scene about anything. Not even pulling her daughter out of university and marrying her off to avoid bankruptcy. Even then all she'd done was pat Maria's hand and say, 'Your father knows best, dear.'

And anyway, if Maria *did* know how to be a great wife and mother, why would she be in this position? Estranged from the man she loved because he could never love her back?

'I'm not sure that I do,' she murmured.

Seb's arm was around her shoulders in less than a heartbeat. 'Maria, I've seen you with Frankie—before, and now. Trust me, you're a wonderful mother.'

'Even though I took him away from his father?' And there it was. The guilt that had eaten away at her every single day of the last year.

Did she even *deserve* Seb's love now? Maria was well aware that leaving him, and taking Frankie, might have ruined any chance of him loving her, ever.

He still wanted her back; she knew that. But how much of that was pride, or comfort and ease, and how much actual affection?

Seb looked away, out over the serene mountains. 'I... I understand, I think, why you went. More than I did, anyway. And, no, I don't like it. But maybe understanding is a good place to start.'

'Maybe it is.' Maybe this was what had been missing before.

Maybe they just needed to understand each other better. And hope that once they understood, they still liked, or even loved, each other.

It was possible.

'But I need you to know…you're not the only one who's changed this last year,' Seb said.

Maria looked at him in surprise, before realising that *of course* he would have changed. He might seem exactly the same as he'd always been on the outside, but his whole life had been turned upside down over the last twelve months.

'I know.'

Seb shook his head. 'I don't think you do. I don't think *I* realised how much I'd changed until last night, when I saw you and Frankie again.'

She'd never heard him talk like this before— open and emotional and honest to a fault. That in itself was evidence he wasn't the man she'd left. But she needed more. 'Tell me?'

Seb sighed, taking a moment to find the words. Maria waited.

'When Frankie turned away from me last night… I can't explain the loss I felt. The guilt and the pain. It was like a stab to the heart. I realised in an instant how much I'd missed, not even just this last year but before that, when I'd come home from the office after he was asleep and leave before he was awake. I've missed so much, Maria, and I know I can never get it back.'

Blinking away unexpected tears, Maria placed her hand over his again, holding on tight. But she didn't interrupt. She needed to hear all of this.

'And it got me thinking about my parents, and Leo. How much they missed—his whole life, really. But not through any choice of their own, or Leo's. They'd have been together if they could. And I just couldn't bear the thought that I could blink and Frankie would be all grown up, too, and I'd have missed it all. Not when there's still something I can do about it.'

He turned to her, staring down into her eyes, and she could feel the truth and the hurt behind his words.

'Losing my parents, finding Leo… It turned my world upside down—even more than you leaving with Frankie. I couldn't be the same person any more after that, Maria. I'm a different man from the one you married. But I hope I can be one you like and respect more. One who can give you the partnership—the marriage—you need.'

Seb's arm was still around her shoulders, warm and solid and reassuring. And it would be, oh, so easy to just sink into his embrace. To accept his promises of change and fall back into her old life again. But for all they'd talked more in the last few hours than they had in the eighteen months or more before she'd left, Maria couldn't help but acknowledge how much more ground they had to cover.

She turned away.

The horses trotted on, heading back from the silent hills into Mont Coeur, and Maria knew that they weren't going to fix things with just one date. Maybe Seb had changed enough to be a better father. She certainly hoped so.

But the question still remained: could they *really* fix their marriage?

'Maria?' Seb whispered her name like snowflakes on the breeze, soft and fragile, as if he didn't want her to blow away. 'I want to get this right. I want to get back to where we used to be.'

His words were colder than the ice wind. Because wasn't that just the problem? The point at which he'd been happiest—when they were married, had Frankie, were living together, and he could have his work and his easy family life— was when she'd felt most lost and alone. When she'd felt unloved and unlovable, and he hadn't even noticed. Even if he *had* changed, would that feeling ever go away without his love?

Did she really want to go back to that? Never.

'I don't want to go backwards,' she said, her voice sharp. 'If I give you another chance—*if*, Seb—then I want it to be because we're moving forward to something new.'

A new family dynamic maybe. Because as much as she needed to protect her heart, she needed to protect Frankie, too. To give him the family—and maybe now the father—that he needed. She couldn't put her own feelings above her son's happiness. She just couldn't.

'And are you? Giving me another chance?' Seb was so close now that if the sleigh jolted even slightly she'd be in his arms, kissing him. She could feel the warmth of his breath against her cheek, could see the hope in those green eyes she knew so well.

She pulled back. 'I don't know yet. Let me sleep on it?'

Disappointment flared in Seb's eyes, but he covered it quickly. He wasn't used to not getting what he wanted, Maria thought before she realised that was wrong. He just wasn't used to things not going to plan, to not getting what he *worked* for.

But she wasn't a business deal, and their family wasn't a merger he could manage through contracts and a good business plan.

Unless…unless that was the only way to get Seb to understand what she needed from him—what *Frankie* needed from him—while still protecting her heart.

He'd said he wanted them to be a family again. And maybe, just maybe, she could live without his love as long as she knew she had his respect, his partnership, and that he valued their family above his work.

It wasn't the dream, but it was close. And in

twelve months away—not to mention all the years before that—she'd never met a man who made her heart beat like Sebastian Cattaneo did.

She owed it to Frankie to try to save their marriage, if it could be saved. She owed him a chance to be with his father.

And if it didn't work, at least she could walk away guilt-free, knowing she'd given it everything she could. Knowing that Frankie would be happier with two parents who loved him but not each other, because *she* would be happier, too. And Seb would have the chance to find someone he *could* love.

She'd know, at least. As much as it might hurt. She'd know that seeking her own future was the right path—the one thing in the last year she'd never quite been certain of.

'You have an alarming look on your face,' Seb observed, from the other side of the sleigh. 'Like you're plotting my downfall.'

'Shh,' Maria said. 'I'm thinking.'

And, besides, he was only partly right. Yes, she was plotting.

But she was plotting *survival*, not downfall. And if she could figure out a way to get this right, they could *both* get what they needed.

Or close, anyway. And sometimes good enough could be enough, right?

CHAPTER SEVEN

'Okay, I've slept on it.'

Seb blinked blurry eyes in the half-light of early morning. If it even was morning. It felt like the middle of the night.

'What time is it?' he asked, pushing himself up onto one elbow.

It must have been his imagination—or maybe he was still dreaming—but he could have sworn that Maria actually stared at his bare chest for a moment, when the sheets fell down. But seconds later she was focused on his face again, her arms folded across her pyjama top, a determined look on her face.

He knew that look. It was the one she'd worn when she'd left him.

He hated that look.

'It's morning,' Maria said, unconvincingly.

Seb glanced at his phone on the bedside table. Five thirty-five. 'Barely.'

'Frankie will be up in less than an hour, and I wanted to talk to you first.'

Seb smiled at the mention of his son. They'd returned from their sleigh ride the afternoon before to find Frankie bouncing with excitement and desperate to tell them all about the fun he'd had with Aunt Noemi and Uncle Max. Max had looked exhausted and Noemi a little triumphant, but the important thing was the babysitting had been a success—even if the date hadn't given him *quite* the victory he'd been looking for.

Frankie had fallen asleep at the dinner table, and Maria had never returned from putting him to bed. Alone, as she'd insisted.

Seb had hoped that meant she was 'sleeping on it'—her decision about their future, that was.

And it seemed he'd been right.

Shuffling up to lean against the headboard, he patted the bed. 'Sit down, at least, if we're going to talk. You're making my neck ache looking up at you.'

Maria looked conflicted, but eventually perched on the end of his bed. It wasn't *quite* how he wanted her there, but if it meant they were making progress towards her staying, he'd take it.

'So. You've slept on it. And?' Seb tried to sound relaxed about the whole thing, when in reality his heart was thumping against his ribs. This could be it. His whole future, in one conversation.

'You said yesterday that you were more comfortable with the requirements of business than the business of being a family, yes?' Maria's crisp delivery made him wonder if she'd been rehearsing these lines all night. Probably, knowing Maria. They may have had very different upbringings in lots of ways, but one thing they had in common was that both sets of parents had instilled in them a chronic fear of messing up.

He hadn't thought about that when she'd left. How hard it must have been for her to go back to her parents and admit that she couldn't make the marriage work. Whether it was fair or not, the Rossis would have seen that as a failure.

How unhappy must she have truly been to choose that over a life with him?

Maria was still staring at him. He quickly ran her last statement through his mind again. 'Yes. I guess so. Sorry, I'm still half-asleep here.'

She bit her lip, and suddenly Seb lost all attention again, unable to focus on anything except her luscious mouth and how much he wanted to kiss it.

Until Maria said, 'In which case, I think we should make a business plan for our marriage,' and he came jolting back to the here and now.

'What?' Surely he hadn't heard that right.

'A business plan. For our marriage.' She said it more slowly this time, as if that would make it a more sensible suggestion.

'Like…with profit-and-loss statements? Or expected sales and markets?' He spent his working days—which was basically all of them—staring at those. Now he had to spend his family time doing it as well?

'With objectives and goals for the marriage. And commitments,' Maria added.

'I thought we made those when we took our wedding vows,' Seb pointed out. He refrained from mentioning the part where she'd run away and broken them, which he figured was pretty good of him under the circumstances.

They'd already *made* a deal. Their whole marriage was a business arrangement. So why did they need a new one?

'Well, clearly just *promising* to love, honour and cherish wasn't enough,' Maria snapped. 'So this time how about we do it your way?'

'My way? This is your idea—how is it *my* way?'

Except…hadn't he realised just yesterday that he hadn't chased his family goal the way his parents had? That he needed to focus on what mattered by keeping it front and centre, like he would any work goal?

'Because you're the one who—' She broke off and took a deep breath, and Seb was almost certain she was counting to ten under her breath. Yeah, that wasn't a great sign. 'Look, Seb, I'm trying to find a way to make this work. It would help if you just went along with me, rather than arguing.'

'It would help if I had coffee,' Seb muttered, scrubbing a hand over his head. He had to try. If nothing else, between now and Christmas Day he had to try literally *anything* that might help him save his marriage.

Even this. 'Okay. I'm listening. I'm open to ideas. Tell me how this would work.'

It had seemed so obvious when she'd come up with the idea. Seb knew business, so she'd turn their relationship into something he understood. And by setting the parameters herself, it gave her control over things, the better to protect her heart this time. It was perfect.

That was the problem with middle-of-the-night epiphanies—they always seemed like a good idea at the time.

But then you had to explain them to your half-asleep estranged husband at stupid o'clock in the morning, and the whole thing fell apart.

No. This was a good idea. More to the point, it was her *only* idea. If she wanted to either turn this marriage into something she could live with or be able to leave again knowing she'd given it her best, they had to follow the plan.

Once she'd explained it in terms that Seb was capable of understanding before coffee.

She contemplated actually going and fetching him coffee before she continued, but it had taken her half the night to get up the confidence to do this in the first place. She couldn't stop now.

He'd just have to struggle through un-caffeinated.

'When our fathers insisted we get married, what was their reasoning?' she said, hoping to get his mind on the same track hers was. Maybe everything only seemed obvious to her because she'd already been living with the basics since she'd first had the idea the previous afternoon. She had to take Seb through the same thought process she'd followed.

'It was…well, I guess it was a business deal.' He sounded slightly embarrassed about it, which was sweet. But it was the truth, and she'd never been under any illusions otherwise. How could she have been?

Her father had been very clear about his hopes for her future, ever since she'd become a teenager. She'd just never taken it seriously until it was too late.

When, at fourteen, she'd brought a boy home from school—not even a boyfriend, just a boy who had been a friend—he'd almost hit the roof. Her mother had calmed him down, though, and then, the next day, she'd been summoned to her father's study.

'You need to understand that you are not free to make any sort of…alliances, specifically of a romantic nature,' he'd said. 'We need more from you than just some boy you pick up from school.'

Slowly, it had dawned on her that, as a daughter, she was useless to him—or to his business. Except in one way. The right marriage. That was all her father was interested in for her—marrying her off to the highest bidder.

She'd railed against it, of course, had wanted to rebel, even—ineffectual as it might have been. Until the day her father had shown up at her university to take her away and dash all her dreams.

Except then he'd told her he needed her to marry Sebastian Cattaneo and, suddenly, against the odds, she'd started to hope again.

Now here she was, all these years later, still clinging to that hope.

Maria swallowed the memories, and tried to get her mind back on track. Their marriage, the business deal.

'Your father's business was failing, but he didn't just want a buyout from Cattaneo Jewels. He wanted a merger,' Seb went on.

'A very physical one, since it involved me putting on a wedding dress.'

'I suppose.' Seb sounded doubtful, but that was *exactly* what they'd agreed to. Two families, and two businesses, brought together into one.

'And I got to thinking last night…maybe the mistake was trying to make this marriage something it isn't.' Or, in her case, letting herself hope it could be something more, then feeling heartbroken when it hadn't happened.

She'd known ever since her father had taken her away from the degree course she'd adored that love was off the table for her. She shouldn't have allowed herself to think otherwise, even for a moment.

Which wasn't to say Seb hadn't made mistakes, too. Ones she hoped her plan would help him rectify.

'Maria, I didn't just marry you because it was good business. You know that, right?' Seb asked, and Maria nodded her head.

'Of course I do. You married me because your father told you to.' Blunt but honest, that was the only way they were going to get through this. Get it all out in the open.

Except for the part about her falling stupidly in love with him, of course. What good would telling him *that* do? Besides, she couldn't bear to see the pity in his eyes when he realised the truth.

'That's not—' Seb cut himself off, rubbing at his eyes. She wished he'd pull the sheet up—his naked torso was simply too distracting for a conversation of this magnitude. Unfortunately, the chalet's state-of-the-art heating system meant that while she was uncomfortably hot in her thick sweater, he was likely to remain half-naked for a while.

Which was a bad thing, she reminded her treacherous body. A *bad* thing.

'We were a team, Maria. We *were*. I married you because I respect you, and more than that, I *like* you. And I don't like many people.' He looked at her balefully, and Maria felt a little of that guilt dripping back in. 'It may not have been a conventional romance, or falling head over heels in love or any of that. But our marriage wasn't nothing either.'

'I never said it was.' Sighing, Maria shifted to sit a little more fully on the bed, holding a hand out to him. He took it after a moment, and her shoulder muscles relaxed just a bit. 'Seb, if this marriage meant nothing to me, I wouldn't be trying so hard to save it.' Yes, she'd walked out. But she'd come back when he'd asked. That had to count for something.

'Okay, then.' Seb squeezed her hand then let it go. 'So, what do we do?'

'Like I said, we need a plan. Like you would for any business partnership you were entering into.' She sucked in a breath, then tried to get back on script. She'd spent half the night rehearsing it, after all. It would be a shame not to use it. 'I think part of the problem was that we went into the marriage—and parenthood, come to that—with different expectations. And we never talked about them, never discussed what we both wanted out of it.'

'And now we should?'

'And now we should.' Seb still didn't look entirely convinced. 'Think about it, Seb. What could it hurt? The worst that happens is that we realise that what we each want is incompatible, and that it can't work out between us.'

'So you walk away again and take Frankie with you?' Seb said.

'So we sit down and figure out a way forward that keeps us *both* in Frankie's life,' Maria corrected him. 'I don't want to take your son away from you, Seb. He needs you, and he deserves you in his life. But you have to make space for him, too. It can't just be video calls at eleven o'clock at night, you know. That's not fatherhood.'

He had the decency to look shamefaced at that. 'I know, I know. So I guess that's one point for our hypothetical agreement, then?'

Maria nodded. 'Only there's nothing hypothetical about this. We're going to write it all down, sign and agree it, then live by it.'

'In that case, I'm definitely going to need coffee,' Seb groaned.

But he wasn't saying no. That was definitely progress. Maria grinned. Maybe they could make time for caffeine. It might help.

'Then let's get some coffee. And my laptop.'

'I want Frankie to know me.' Seb met Maria's gaze over their coffee mugs and the kitchen counter, as her fingers hovered over the keyboard of her laptop. 'That's my number one, nonnegotiable point. I want him to be as happy and comfortable spending time with me as he is with you.'

Maria glanced across at the baby monitor between them on the counter before answering. Frankie was still asleep—mostly because it was still insanely early—and Seb couldn't help but feel that was for the best. With any luck, his parents would have ironed out all the wrinkles in his future and he'd have his family back by the time he woke up.

If Maria agreed to what he needed. And if she didn't ask for anything too unreasonable in return.

Now he had coffee, Seb had to admit this whole idea wasn't as stupid as he'd first thought. A marriage—any marriage, not just a convenient business one like theirs—*was* basically a merger, in lots of ways. And Maria was right. He knew how to handle those.

He could do this. He was almost certain.

He definitely had to give it his best shot.

'Seb… I can't give you that.' Maria sounded apologetic, which wasn't going to stop him arguing the point. But she put a hand up to stop him before he could even start. 'No, let me explain. I'm not saying I'll keep Frankie away from you or anything like that. I'm saying that your relationship with your son is down to *you*. And him, of course, but you're the adult here, so mostly you.'

Seb stared down at his coffee. She had a point. Even before she'd flown back to Italy to her parents' estate, he hadn't exactly put the time in with Frankie. He'd been more concerned with building up a successful business for his son to inherit one day than with spending time with him.

Somehow, there had to be time for both. He might have to give up sleep, but it had to be possible. What was the point otherwise? It might have taken him a while—and some huge life changes—to realise how important all those individual moments with his son were, but now that he had he wasn't going to carry on making the same mistakes.

He'd already lost enough of Frankie's childhood. And he couldn't let Frankie grow up not knowing his father, like Leo had.

'Okay. I take your point—I need to make the time for Frankie. But it would be a lot easier to do that if we were living in the same house. I want to be able to come home from work at the end of the day and hang out with him.' And, yeah, okay, so then maybe he'd put in another couple of hours in the home office after Frankie was asleep—because it wasn't as if he could just give up all his responsibilities overnight. But he could rebalance them—if Maria worked with him on that.

She gave a slow nod, but somehow it didn't feel like an agreement. 'I think that's going to depend on the rest of this document, don't you?' she said. 'I mean, if we can find a compromise that makes us both happy…'

'You'll stay,' he finished for her. But there was no nod this time. Seb gripped the handle of his mug a little tighter. 'Maria, that's why I'm doing this. Why I'm sitting here at godforsaken o'clock in the morning writing a *business proposal* for my life. What's the point of it if you don't stay at the end?'

'I'm not saying I won't!' Maria protested, although he could hear the reluctance in her voice. That was *exactly* what she meant. 'I'm just saying that there's a lot more we need to agree on first.'

Seb shook his head, anger rising up in him as the caffeine settled into his bloodstream. 'No. Frankie is what matters most—I thought we could at least both agree on that.'

'Of course we do!'

'Then I need a promise from you, before we go any further,' Seb said, his voice harsh, even to his own ears. 'If I agree to whatever plan you come up with here—'

'*We* come up with,' Maria corrected him, as if she honestly believed he wasn't just following her lead. That he wouldn't say yes to *anything* if it kept her and Frankie there with him.

'Fine, that *we* come up with. If I agree to it, if I keep to it between now and Christmas, you have to stay. You have to give us a real chance to make our marriage work again.'

Maria's eyes were huge. 'You mean, if you really make time for our family, for Frankie, and everything else… I move back here?'

'If I don't mess things up over the next two weeks between now and Christmas. Yes.' Was he being unreasonable? Seb wasn't sure. But Maria had been right about one thing—he knew business. And the most important thing in business was being able to negotiate hard.

'I'm not—'

'I need an answer, Maria, otherwise there's no point going any further with this.' Ruthless, that was the key. There was no room for weakness in business. Or marriage, it seemed.

He could see the conflicting arguments playing out in her head, showing on her face as clearly as if she'd said them out loud. He waited, ignoring the gnawing feeling of wrongness about treating his wife this way that ate away at his stomach.

She'd wanted their marriage to be all business. He was only giving her what she'd asked for.

'Fine,' she snapped eventually. 'But you have to meet every condition we set. Every rule we make. If you mess up… I don't believe in third chances, Sebastian.'

'Right.' Seb gave a sharp nod. 'In that case, let's get down to specifics. I'm guessing you have a list? Things you need from me?'

'Actually…yes,' Maria admitted.

'Good. Because I've got some of my own to add, too.' Or he would have, by the time it was his turn to dictate terms. He just had to think of them first. After all, she'd had a twelve-hour head start on this one. 'Let's get started.'

This would be easy. Just like setting quarterly goals at work. He never missed those. He wouldn't miss these.

How could he, when the stakes were so much higher?

'Okay, then,' Maria said. 'Point One A…'

Seb reached for the coffee pot. He had a feeling this could take a while.

CHAPTER EIGHT

'WAIT—YOU PUT together a business plan for your *marriage*?' Noemi stared at her incredulously as they stood together on the chalet's sprawling wooden porch. Maria hoped that she could blame the icy air for the way her cheeks turned pink. It hadn't sounded nearly so crazy until Noemi had said it *that* way.

'Seb's a businessman,' she explained to her sister-in-law. 'I figured I needed to talk to him in terms he understood—and, well, this is what I came up with.'

And it had worked, hadn't it? It might have taken them most of the morning, but they had an actual plan, with commitments and objectives, all typed up, printed in triplicate, and signed by both of them. They'd each kept a copy, and the third had been stored away in the chalet's fireproof safe, hidden behind the fake bookcase in the snug.

'If we're doing this, we're doing this properly,' Seb had said as he'd locked it away.

Maria was just grateful that Frankie had decided to sleep in again. Apparently the cold, crisp air was tiring him out. Well, that and his aunts and uncles—who had taken over entertaining him while she and Seb had finished their negotiations.

Noemi surveyed her over the mug of peppermint tea in her hands. 'I guess that makes some sort of twisted sense. If you're you and Seb.'

'What exactly does that mean?' Maria asked, even though she had a suspicion she already knew.

Noemi shrugged. 'Just that... I don't know. It's not like your marriage was a conventional one from the start, was it?'

'We were a means to an end. A merger marriage to save my father's pride and money.' Her tone was a little too bitter for Maria to pretend it didn't still sting, but then, Noemi knew that anyway. She knew *her*.

'But you were friends first for a really long time,' Noemi reminded her. 'I mean, I know I was younger, but you and Seb always seemed so close, and I was always trailing around behind you both. Honestly, I can't remember a time you didn't feel like part of our family already.'

Tears pricked at Maria's eyes. The Cattaneos *had* been family. All of them, not just Seb. Returning to her parents' estate should have felt like going home. But it hadn't, not at all. 'Apart from the time I walked out and left you all, you mean?'

'No.' Noemi shook her head emphatically, her gorgeous hair swaying in the breeze. 'You were still family. You'll always be family, I hope you know that. Whatever happens with you and Seb, you'll always be my sister.'

Maria groped for Noemi's hand, squeezing it tight. 'Thank you.'

Noemi squeezed back, then let her go, smiling a little too brightly. 'So. What does my miserable brother have to do to keep up his end of the deal?'

Putting her mug of coffee—her sixth cup of the day, she suspected, but to be honest, she'd stopped counting at this point—down on the rail that ran around the porch, Maria ticked off the basic terms of their agreement on her fingers.

'The main thing is that he has to show me that his family is more important than his business.' Noemi raised her eyebrows at that, but Maria carried on anyway. 'He needs to include me in his life—personal and work—so that we feel like a true partnership again. He needs to spend time with Frankie—playing, reading him stories, putting him to bed, that sort of thing. He needs to learn Frankie's routine and work with it. He needs to parent according to our agreed methods, and not undermine all the work I've been doing with Frankie over the last year. He needs to talk to me before making any big decisions about his time—like lengthy business trips overseas, that sort of thing. And he needs to come up with a plan for an actual family holiday next year—no laptops, no mobile phones, just the three of us together.'

It sounded like quite a lot, put like that, Maria

supposed, but really, weren't these things that any good father and husband should be doing *anyway*?

Noemi gave a low whistle. 'They are some lofty goals, my friend. I hope he can live up to them.'

'So do I,' Maria said, and realised that she meant it. Even if it meant she spent the rest of her life with a husband who would never love her the way she loved him, if she could have all that—if *Frankie* could have all that—she'd be content. She hoped.

'And it explains the current ski lesson.' Noemi tilted her head out towards the snowy ground in front of the chalet, where Sebastian was currently explaining to a snowsuited Frankie all about the mechanics and physics of skiing.

Maria was pretty sure Frankie wasn't getting much of it, but he seemed happy enough to be out in the snow with his father, all the same. That was something.

'I have to say, though,' Noemi went on, drawing her attention back, 'nothing about this plan of yours exactly screams "romance".'

'Why would it?' Maria asked. 'Like I said, we're a business partnership. Covering that up with roses and love songs doesn't change that.' And it only gave her false hope. She needed to be totally clear about what this was. A merger of their two families, and businesses, to support and nurture their child, who would grow up to inherit a share in them. Not a love story—a business contract.

It was the only way she could protect her heart if she decided to stay.

'Hmm.' Noemi didn't look convinced. 'Okay, so I've heard your demands for Seb. What did he ask of you?'

Maria resisted the urge to wince. She'd been hoping her sister-in-law wouldn't ask her that. 'Oh, you know. Regular debrief meetings over dinner without Frankie.'

'You mean date nights,' Noemi translated, sounding delighted. Maria ignored her. As long as she said they were meetings, they were meetings. Even if Seb had suggested they go back to the restaurant where they'd had lunch yesterday for the first one. But at night this time, so they could dress up and maybe go dancing afterwards.

Still, a meeting. Not a date. They'd had one of those now. How many more did they need?

She went back to her list.

'That he and Frankie get to have a boys' day every so often, just the two of them.'

'Aw, that's sweet.' It was, Maria had to agree. It was also slightly unnerving. It had been just her and Frankie for so long. The idea of letting his father take him off to do who knew what felt alien and strange.

'And that the three of us come to Ostania to visit you and Max, the moment those babies are born.'

Noemi pressed a hand to her bump, her eyes huge in her beautiful face. 'He said that? He wrote that into your contract?'

'He did.' Maria smiled. She knew that Noemi and Sebastian's relationship had been strained recently, maybe since before she'd left, but certainly since their parents' deaths and the will reading that had put Leo in charge of the business. If her return could go any small way to helping mend the rift between the siblings, it only made it more worthwhile.

'Then I can't wait for that.' Noemi beamed back at her, all sunlight on the snow and pure, unadulterated happiness.

Maria tried to ignore the envy bubbling in the pit of her stomach, and turned her attention back to Frankie and Seb, just in time to see Leo and Anissa walking up the path. As she watched, Leo bent over, scooped up a handful of snow, packed it between his hands, then lobbed it at the back of Seb's head.

Maria bit her lip as she waited to see how her husband would react. He'd never had a brother before—neither of them had—and he'd never responded well to teasing, or anything that made him look a fool. Even as a child he'd hated it—

although when they'd been younger he'd some-times played the clown to make her laugh, if it was just the two of them. But never in front of anyone else, and never since he'd taken on the business mantle of being Salvo's successor.

And for Leo to do it in front of Frankie...

But suddenly a deep, warm laugh rang over the snow, echoing back from the hills, and she saw Seb kneeling in the snow, making snowballs for Frankie to lob back at 'Uncle Leo'.

'Wow,' Noemi said. 'I didn't expect that.'

'Neither did I,' Maria said, faintly, watching as Anissa came and joined Seb and Frankie's side, all three of them teaming up to pelt Leo with snow. 'Not ever.'

Maybe Seb was right. Maybe he really had been changed by the recent turmoil in his life.

Seb hoisted Frankie up onto his shoulders to give him the height advantage, and gamely took more snowballs to the chest from Leo as Anissa supplied Frankie with his own ammunition. They all laughed and shouted and joked, and even from a distance Maria could see the joy on her son's face.

This was what she'd wanted for him. This was why she'd come back.

For family. Because however helpful and polite her mother might have been since she'd moved home, it couldn't make up for her father's cold glares and mumbled complaints. And she knew from her own childhood that their house could never provide the loving family relationship she wanted for Frankie.

She'd do her best alone, of course, and that could be enough. But why should he have to settle for just her when he could have all this?

As Seb turned and grinned at her, his cheeks pink and his eyes bright, for the first time Maria believed that maybe this could really work.

Because the Seb she'd left would never have had a snowball fight with a two-year-old. Would never have let himself appear so relaxed and uncaring about his reputation.

The Seb she'd left would have been stuck in his office and never even made it outside in the first place.

'Maybe he really has changed,' she murmured, the thought settled in her mind at last.

'Maybe he has,' Noemi agreed, sounding every bit as astonished as Maria felt. 'Who knew? Christmas miracles really do happen.'

The minute the first snowball hit him, Seb had his usual, instinctive response to anything unexpected or unwelcome—to turn and yell first, then give whoever had attacked him the trademark Sebastian glare until he or she went away. Then Frankie had giggled, and he'd realised that his usual instincts were what had got him into this mess in the first place.

Seb turned and saw his new brother and his girlfriend waiting for his reaction. It also didn't escape his notice that Leo had another snowball packed down in his hand, ready to attack.

This was war, then.

'Throw one back, Papà! Throw another snowball!' Frankie cried, and Seb laughed—sudden and true and deep. Pure instinct and happiness.

When had he last laughed like that? Had he ever?

He couldn't remember. Which probably said more than it didn't.

So Seb bent down and made snowballs for his son to throw at his uncle, and wondered how it had taken him thirty-two years to find this kind of contentment.

Wondered how he could keep it now that he had.

The afternoon fell into a flurry of snow attacks and laughter, Anissa abandoning Leo to assist Seb and Frankie in their fight. Seb hoisted his son onto his shoulders, barely even feeling the snowballs Leo tossed at him—obviously, Uncle Leo would never throw them at Frankie, but Seb was perfectly fair game.

Somewhere in between flying snowballs Seb turned towards the chalet and saw Maria and

Noemi watching them, both smiling. And then all he saw was Maria's eyes, and the hope that flared in them.

He was doing something right. But he knew, in a sudden blinding flash like sunlight on ice, it wasn't going to be enough.

He could meet every target in her business plan, achieve every goal she set him. But it still wouldn't be enough.

Because he didn't *want* a business partnership. He wanted a marriage, a family. A connection.

And even he knew that took more than a signed contract.

But how did he convince Maria of that?

Two hours later, the sun was starting to slip below the mountains, and they had all taken refuge back in the chalet to warm up. Leo slapped Seb on the back as he ran a towel over his soaking wet hair.

'No hard feelings, brother?' Leo asked, and Seb was sure he could hear just a hint of anxiety in his question.

He flashed Leo a reassuring smile. 'I was just wondering if this is what it would have been like to grow up with you.'

Leo grinned back. 'Oh, I expect it would have been much worse.'

'I think it's so lovely you're both reliving the childhood you missed out on,' Noemi said drily.

'Because two more children is absolutely what we need around here.'

'I'd have thought it was good practice for you,' Seb joked, and she rolled her eyes.

'Do you want to get a drink? We could go into town, check out that new bar that opened,' Leo suggested, and for moment something inside Seb longed to say yes. To hang out with his new brother and build on this tentative relationship they'd been building.

But there was another relationship he had to tend to first.

'Another night?' he suggested. 'I want to help Maria get Frankie to bed. Poor little guy was exhausted.' Frankie might not have learned a whole lot about skiing that afternoon, but he'd certainly had a lot of fun.

And maybe he'd learned something about family, too. Maybe they both had.

'Another night,' Leo confirmed, patting him on the shoulder again as he headed across the room towards Anissa.

Slinging the damp towel over his shoulder, Sebastian headed up the stairs to the master suite to find his wife and child.

He heard them before he saw them—the squealing and splashing leading him straight to the large bathroom attached to the master suite. Leaning against the doorpost, he watched as Maria paraded a series of ducks along the edge of the over-sized bathtub. Frankie waited until they were all lined up just right, then swept an arm across to knock them all into the water, giggling manically as he did so.

'He still likes his bath, then,' he observed. That was something he remembered from when Frankie had been a baby—how he'd loved to splash about in the water when it came to bath time. Not that he'd often been there to see it, but some nights, if he'd got home early, he'd caught the end of it.

He'd loved those nights. Why hadn't he tried harder to make sure there were more of them?

Sometimes it felt like the man who had lost Maria, who had lived through that awful last argument and watched her walk away, was a totally different person. With a year's distance, he couldn't understand why he hadn't seen the same things then that he knew in his heart now. How much Maria mattered to him. How every moment with Frankie was precious.

How his marriage was something to be grateful for every day.

Maria started slightly at the sound of his voice, but turned to look at him with an easy enough smile. 'He *definitely* still loves his bath. Almost as much as it seems he likes snowball fights.'

Seb couldn't help but grin as he thought about

the afternoon they'd spent together. 'He did seem to enjoy it, didn't he?'

'We have snowball fight again, Papà?' Frankie asked, looking up from his ducks.

'Maybe tomorrow, *piccolo*,' Seb replied. 'For now, I think it must be nearly your bedtime.'

'Would you like Papà to read you your bedtime story?' Maria asked. Frankie nodded enthusiastically, and Seb thought his heart might burst at the sight.

This. This was what mattered. This was *all* that mattered.

And he'd do whatever the contract with Maria said if it made sure he kept it for ever.

For ever would give him time to convince her that this wasn't just business between them. It was family.

CHAPTER NINE

'I THINK HE'S ASLEEP,' Seb whispered, as he padded through the doorway from the room she and Frankie shared, leaving the door a little open. 'His eyes were closing all through that last story.'

'How many did you read him?' Maria asked.

'Um, four? Maybe five?' Seb shrugged. 'He just kept handing me books, so I just kept reading them.'

Maria rolled her eyes—mostly to stop herself smiling besottedly at the husband she'd designated as nothing more than a business partner. 'He's normally only allowed two.' But Frankie loved his stories, so would keep going as long as someone would read them to him.

Seb shrugged again, sinking onto the sofa beside him. 'Well, I've missed out on a lot of bedtime stories. I figure I have ground to make up.'

And how was she supposed to argue with that?

'I made some hot chocolate for us,' she said instead, motioning to the mugs on the coffee table in front of the roaring fire. 'Figured you might still need warming up a bit after your snowy adventures earlier.'

'I love hot chocolate,' Seb said, reaching for his mug. 'Oh, and you even added marshmallows!'

'Of course. I didn't forget everything while I was away, you know.' She hadn't forgotten anything. But he didn't need to know that.

The smile Seb gave her was just a little bit sad. It made Maria wonder if they'd ever manage a conversation that didn't somehow come back to how she'd left him. If they'd ever move forward beyond that fact.

Maybe eventually. If she stayed long enough this time. And if Seb kept up the way he'd been that afternoon, she might have to.

He certainly seemed to be going all out so far to meet every expectation and objective she'd set him. If she'd realised sooner that this was the way to get cooperation from her husband she'd have tried it years ago.

But if he kept going on the way he had today, Maria would have to uphold her end of the bargain, too. She'd have to recommit to their business partnership marriage and stay, something that somehow both terrified and excited her.

They hadn't set time limits on what would happen after Christmas. If he met his objectives until Christmas, she'd stay and give their marriage a second chance. It didn't mean she couldn't leave again if he reverted back to the old Seb.

If she could pluck up the courage and steel her heart to leave him twice, that was. Something Maria wasn't at all sure about.

She remembered the winter she'd come home from college at twenty to visit the Cattaneos—just five months before she'd left university for good. She'd had two full years since she'd left home of trying to forget about Seb, and the way he made her feel. To forget his smile, or his hand in hers as they'd skated on the ice. To forget the way he'd look at her across the dinner table when her father said something awful, just to let her know he was on her side. To forget how hard her fifteen-year-old self had fallen for him.

He'd been away studying in London, and between that and starting work at his father's company, it had been easy to avoid him, especially with her own studies and friends to keep her occupied. To be honest, it had grown almost embarrassing to be mooning after him. Even if no one ever said anything, Maria had never been able to shake the feeling that they all *knew*, and were laughing at her behind her back. What was cute at fifteen or sixteen was frankly humiliating at nineteen or twenty.

It had been easier to stay out of his way, entertain herself flirting with other boys, work hard for a degree she cared deeply about, and build her own life. By the end of her first year at university she'd almost convinced herself that what she'd thought she'd felt for Seb had only been a childhood crush.

Then she'd seen Sebastian again for the first time in two years.

He'd been standing in the snow with his father, waiting for her, the winter sun glinting off his short dark hair. And he'd smiled, and she'd fallen all over again, harder than ever.

She'd broken away from Seb once before, only to fall deeper in love when she'd come back. And now she was afraid history might be about to repeat itself—but she had no idea how to stop it.

Maybe it was already too late.

'So, how did I do with our contract today?' Seb asked, breaking through her memories. 'Am I keeping up my end of the bargain?'

'I think we could definitely say that.' Maria reached for her own hot chocolate, thinking how happy, how *young* Sebastian had looked, playing in the snow with Frankie and Leo. She hadn't seen that Sebastian in a long time. Hadn't realised how much she'd missed him until today.

'In that case…since things are going so well to plan, perhaps we could talk about something?' Seb kept his eyes on the marshmallows bobbing in his hot chocolate as he asked, which made her a little nervous.

Maria frowned. 'Of course. But what, exactly?'

'How do you…?' Seb took a breath and started again, meeting her gaze this time as he spoke. There was a cautious reserve in his eyes. 'If you stay, if I meet all your conditions and you and Frankie stay with me…how do you see that going?'

As if they hadn't already spent the whole morning hammering this out.

'How do you mean? We've talked about this already—you will make time for family as well as business. You'll involve me in your decisions. Do I need to get the contract back out for you to read it again?'

'No, that's not…that's not what I mean.' Seb looked awkwardly around him, as if wishing he'd never started the conversation.

But he had, and now Maria really had to know what he was trying to get at. 'Is this about Frankie?'

Shaking his head, Seb put down his mug and reached for her, taking her hands in his. 'No. It's about us.'

As much as part of him wished he'd never started this conversation, Seb knew it was one they needed to have. He'd known it when they'd been hammering out the terms of their contract over coffee that morning, and he'd known it for certain when he'd seen Maria smiling at him through the snow. He just hadn't been ready to address it until now—alone, in the evening shadows, with a fire and a hot chocolate.

Although a little brandy in the hot chocolate would probably help.

If Maria stayed, he wanted more than a business partner. He wanted his *wife* back. And everything that went with that.

'What I need to know is…what sort of relationship do you see us having in the future, if you come home?' He watched Maria's eyes widen as she realised what he was asking.

'You mean…will our relationship be purely business, or will we resume, um, our physical, well…?' She trailed off, and Seb held back a laugh at the sight of his wife trying to make their sex life part of a business contract.

Then he realised how bad that sounded, and frowned. *That* wasn't what he wanted at all. He didn't want any relationship between them to be an obligation, something agreed on paper that Maria felt she *had* to do.

If he ever had Maria in his bed again, it would only be because she wanted to be there. Because she craved that physical connection between them as much as he did.

And they had connected. *Really* connected.

He may not have had any serious relationships in his life before he'd married Maria, but that didn't mean he was inexperienced. He knew how sex could be with women he was attracted to, liked, and whose company he enjoyed.

None of them had ever come close to sex with Maria.

It wasn't just her beauty, her gorgeous curves, or even the friendship they'd built over the years. There was something more there between them, something he'd never been able to pin down to a single word or phrase.

But it had been real. And it had taken his breath away, from the first time he'd touched her, and every single time since.

He didn't want that perfect memory ruined by trying to make it part of their contract.

'Maybe it's a bad idea to talk about this,' he said abruptly, dropping her hands. Yes, he wanted to know her intentions, but somehow the whole conversation had got twisted around, without ever going anywhere. Maybe he just had to wait until it happened naturally—or didn't happen.

It was just a shame he was so bad with uncertainty.

'No,' Maria said, biting down on her bottom lip. 'You're right. Our physical relationship is an important aspect of our partnership. We *should* discuss it. I mean, we haven't even spoken about whether we'd like Frankie to have a brother or sister one day.'

Another baby. One he could get things right for, from the start. A companion for Frankie, like Noemi had been for him, like Leo could have been, perhaps would be now. Maria had never had a sibling, and he knew she'd been lonely—when she hadn't been with the Cattaneos, anyway. Of course she'd be thinking about this.

And he'd just been thinking about sex. God, no wonder she thought he needed a business plan to just be able to act like a normal human being.

His shock must have shown on his face, because Maria instantly started backtracking. 'But you probably meant something else. Like…if this is a business relationship, are we free to see other people? Recreationally, so to speak.'

See other people? That was basically the *opposite* of what he'd been thinking about.

Did *she* want to see other men? She said she hadn't dated while they'd been apart…but she wouldn't, not with things unsettled between them. He knew Maria.

If she wanted to start a relationship with someone new, she'd make sure she tied up all the loose ends with him first, so she could move on free and clear.

Was that what she wanted? Either to be free of him for ever, or to have an arrangement that gave her enough freedom to seek her own happiness?

Anger and fear and confusion all warred inside him for prominence—until he took a moment to really look at Maria before he responded.

She didn't look like a woman asking for freedom, or looking forward to being able to go out and find a new love. She looked...resigned? As if she thought this was what *he* wanted?

How often had he reacted to Maria without looking before? How much had he missed seeing?

Not this time.

'Maria.' The word came out low, and surely she must hear his desire in it? Well, he'd tell her, just in case. They'd spent too long missing each other's meanings, it seemed. 'Maria, the only woman I ever want to be with is you.'

The surprise on her face was almost comic. But he also saw doubt creeping in behind it. He couldn't have that.

'Believe me, I have no interest in other women, no desire for *anyone* except for my wife. Except for you.' He reached out to tuck a strand of her dark hair behind one ear, cupping her cheek as he did so. 'You have to know you are—and have always been—the most beautiful woman in the world to me.'

'You've never...you never told me that.' Maria stumbled over the words. 'Before.'

Because he was an idiot. Clearly.

'I should have.' He should have told her every day, and would from now on, if it meant she'd stay. 'Because it's true. You're so beautiful you take my breath away. You always have.'

Her cheeks flushed with colour, only making her more beautiful to him.

'So, if I stay…you want us to…'

'I want us to have a marriage, as well as a partnership,' Seb finished for her. 'I want us to have it all.'

Maria could feel the hope rising within her—that same optimism she'd felt after their wedding day. With each day of their honeymoon it had grown that little bit more. The two glorious weeks they'd spent together out in the Seychelles, making the most of just being the two of them, for the first time ever. No family interfering or expecting things from them. No meetings, no calls, no emails. Just them.

It had been one of the happiest times of her life, Maria realised. Learning Sebastian anew as her husband, rather than just a friend of the family. Talking about anything and everything, for hours, just because they could. Spending whole days lazing about on the beach, or splashing through the water, asking questions and listening to the answers.

And at night…that had been a whole different world to explore. It had been the one aspect of their marriage Maria had been most nervous about. After all, she knew that their families and business interests aligned, and had spent enough time with Sebastian growing up to know that they could get along well together, even if they hadn't seen much of each other over the last few years. But beyond a few simple, often observed kisses, they'd never had a chance to test the more *physical* aspects of their compatibility.

But she needn't have worried. From the moment they'd been alone, the first time Seb's lips had met hers, she'd known there were absolutely no concerns at all on that score.

She bit her lip just remembering how he'd made her body feel—like singing and sinking all at once, pleasure taking over in a way she'd never experienced before.

Or since, in fact.

Oh, sure, they'd had sex since they'd returned from honeymoon, but it had always come in second place since then. Seb would be too busy at work, coming to bed hours after she did, or distracted and checking his emails if he was there. They'd managed to conceive Frankie, at least, but ever since the honeymoon was over, Maria had completely understood why people used that saying.

The minute their plane had landed, Seb had been checking his work emails on his phone. And in some ways it felt like he'd barely looked up and seen her again since.

But he was seeing her now. Here, in front of the

fire in the suite they'd shared, their son asleep in the next room, he couldn't take his eyes off her.

He'd said he thought she was the most beautiful woman in the world, and somehow, finally, she believed it. And heaven knew she'd never seen a more gorgeous man than Sebastian Cattaneo. However hard she'd looked.

But it was too soon. So he'd managed one afternoon playing in the snow with Frankie. That wasn't enough for her to give in, to let herself get her hopes up about for ever. That way, she knew from bitter experience, led only to disappointment and heartbreak.

More than once before she'd thought it would be different. After their honeymoon, then when she'd got pregnant with Frankie and Seb had been so attentive she'd thought she'd scream if it wasn't so adorable. Even when Frankie had been born, and Seb had actually managed to make it to the hospital from the boardroom in time to be there and hold her hand—just.

But every time she'd thought she'd won his attention—and maybe even found the path to his love—he'd get distracted again, running off to deal with some sort of work crisis, or to discuss future plans for the business with his father. Anything except stay with her and enjoy their family.

It could still be the same this time. She couldn't

lose sight of that. She needed to protect her heart—and her future.

If she stayed, it would be on her own terms, and without any false expectations. She could mandate that Seb spend time with her and Frankie, she could insist on partnership terms, but she couldn't make Seb fall in love with her.

Which meant she needed other things to make her happy. She had Frankie, of course, and Seb's family, she supposed. The only other thing she craved was a meaningful career. And Seb could give her that, too, if he wanted.

If she asked.

She'd never told him what she needed before, had expected him to know instinctively. And she knew now that didn't work with Seb. If she wanted something, she needed to tell him.

She had to ask.

Pulling back, Maria ignored Seb's disappointed expression and reached for her cooling hot chocolate. 'I hope we can find our way back there in time, too,' she said honestly.

Well, mostly honestly. In truth, she'd let him take her right there on the sofa if she thought it wouldn't end up with her heart getting broken in the morning.

'In time,' Seb repeated, and she supposed she had to give him a few points for not asking how much time.

He knew what he had to do to make her stay. And if he kept doing it…well, Maria suspected it wouldn't be very much time at all before she was also back in his arms and in his bed. She was only human, after all.

And in the meantime…

'I actually wanted to talk to you about something, too. Something more work related.'

Seb arched a sardonic eyebrow. 'I thought the aim of our contract was to get me focusing *less* on work, not more.'

'It is,' Maria agreed. 'But it's also about building our partnership. Finding ways to include each other in our everyday lives.'

'And my everyday life *is* the business,' Seb surmised. 'Fair enough. Ask away.'

Maria sucked in a breath, hoping the air particles included the courage she needed to make her request.

'Do you think…when I've finished my course, do you think there might be a place for me at Cattaneo Jewels?'

Both eyebrows flew up this time. 'You want a *job*?'

'Is that so unbelievable?' Maria snapped, all lust faded now with just four words from him. 'Or I am just so unemployable?'

He waved her argument away with a flap of his hand. 'The company would be lucky to have you.

I was just…surprised. You were always trying to persuade me to spend *less* time at work.'

'Well, maybe if you have help I'll achieve that aim,' she hit back, trying to ignore the warm feeling that had returned when he'd said 'lucky to have you'.

'That's true.' He gave her a half-smile. 'And it would give us something else in common. Something else to draw us together.'

'Exactly.' She beamed back, glad he'd got it.

As a colleague, she'd be more of an equal than ever. *That* was what she wanted most.

Seb sat back, draping an arm across the back of the sofa. 'Well, Cattaneo Jewels is a family business. And you're family. Of course there's a job for you if you want it. And I wasn't kidding— we'd be lucky to have you.'

'Don't you need to ask Leo first?' Maria asked. 'I mean, I know your parents' will left the majority stake to him…' A sensitive subject, she was sure. But Seb seemed relaxed enough for her to broach it now.

To her surprise, his half-smile broadened to a full-on grin. 'Actually, that might be changing. He spoke to me the other day about signing over his shares to me. Giving me control of the company again.'

Maria's eyes widened. 'That's…great.' It was. In lots of ways. It just also meant that Seb had no get-out—no one to share the burden if his family needed him more than the business did.

Seb seemed to guess her concern. Resting a hand against her thigh, he leaned close, gazing directly into her eyes as if to convince her of his honesty. 'I won't let it change anything, Maria. I swear to you. Never mind signed agreements and contracts—*this* is my promise. *Nothing* comes before our family. Not any more. Okay?'

'Okay,' Maria whispered.

And, God help her, she believed him.

CHAPTER TEN

SEBASTIAN GLARED DOWN at the paperwork in front of him. He'd hoped that printing it out would make it easier to digest than staring at it on the screen, but if anything, the last agreement Salvo had worked on in his lifetime was even more complex and concerning in hard copy.

He sighed, returned to the first page and started reading over again.

A soft knock at the door disturbed him after only a few moments, and he looked up as he called, 'Come in.' He knew he should be annoyed at being interrupted, but to be honest, the distraction was welcome. Even more so when Maria's beautiful face appeared around the door.

'Hey.' With a soft smile, she slid into the chair on the opposite side of the desk and peered across at his papers. 'What're you working on?'

'Papà's last deal,' Seb said with a groan. Then he realised. The only time Maria had come to his office at the chalet in the last week had been to fetch him when they had plans to go out. Had he forgotten some plan or another? And if so, what? He checked his watch quickly. 'Sorry, were we supposed to be doing something with Frankie?

I've been lost in these documents for days, it feels like. But I'll stop now and we can—'

'Seb, it's okay.' Maria's smile was almost a grin now. 'Much as I appreciate your efforts to drop everything and spend time with your family, Frankie has been whisked off to the local toy store by his all-too-indulgent aunts and uncles. Apparently it's time for him to choose his Christmas presents.'

'And you didn't want to go?' Seb asked, surprised.

'I was told—quite firmly—by your sister that I wasn't invited.'

Seb bit back a smirk. 'So he's getting spoiled rotten while you're not there to stop them.'

'Basically.'

'Lucky Frankie.' Seb leaned back in his chair, surveying her across the desk. 'So, what are you up to?'

'Absolutely nothing.' Maria made it sound like the worst fate in the world. Whereas, to Sebastian, it sounded much more like an opportunity.

'Then you've got time to do something with me,' he said gleefully.

Maria rolled her eyes and, before he could suggest something romantic and maybe even a little bit seductive, she reached across the desk and picked up the stack of papers he'd been trying to make sense of. Her eyebrows rose steadily as she flicked through it, then started at the beginning again, just as he had.

Okay, so it wasn't romantic, but Seb couldn't help but wonder what Maria would make of the contract. So he waited.

After another minute or two she put the papers back down on the desk. 'I have trouble believing your father wrote that contract.'

'He didn't,' Seb confirmed. 'It was the other side. What gave it away?'

'It's convoluted, confusing and unclear in areas that are likely going to blow up on you later on.'

Exactly what Seb had been worried about. 'Want to help me figure out how to fix it?'

Maria beamed. 'Absolutely.'

An hour later, any doubts Seb might have had about Maria working for Cattaneo Jewels were definitely long gone. As they worked their way line by line through the deal Salvo had struck, Maria was right there with him—and often a step or two ahead—as they identified ambiguities, potential problems and possible attempts to slip something past them. Occupied with another big project at the time, Seb hadn't been in on the negotiations for the deal—the takeover of a smaller jewellery firm in Switzerland—so trying to second-guess exactly what his father had been aiming for, or had agreed, was tricky. Luckily, Salvo's assistant had taken good notes.

Finally, they reached the end of the document—now covered in scrawled notes and questions in both their handwriting—and Seb sat back, rolling his shoulders to try to release the tension that had settled there.

'You okay?' Maria asked, watching him.

'Yeah. Just glad I had you here to help me with this,' he admitted, 'otherwise it was going to take all night.'

Maria frowned, and pulled out her phone. 'It practically *is* night. Noemi and Max should be back with Frankie by now…' She swiped across the screen of her phone, and her face cleared as she scanned it. 'Except they've gone for ice creams, apparently. Noemi says they'll be back in an hour, and that Frankie has asked them to give him his bath and story tonight.'

'Really?' Seb couldn't help but smile at that. He loved how close Frankie had grown to *all* his family. 'In that case, I guess we've got a little more time to kill.'

'More work?' Maria asked, stretching out her arms in front of her, her fingers interlaced. She must ache as much as he did, but there was no hint of it in her voice.

But Seb was done with work for the day. It was time for some fun. 'I've got a much better idea.'

* * *

Darkness was already falling as Seb led Maria out of the chalet, a mysterious bag slung over his shoulder.

'Are you seriously not going to tell me where we're going?' she asked, picking her way through the snow behind him.

'It's a surprise.' Seb glanced back over his shoulder and flashed her a grin. 'I'm being romantic.'

'That's half the problem,' Maria muttered under her breath, as she followed him.

Distracted, work-focused Seb she was used to. This new version, who showered her with attention, never missed a date and read Frankie his bedtime story every night, was a complete mystery. Working with him on that contract, though…that was new, yes, but the discussion and collaboration was familiar from the first days of their marriage, when Seb had still found time to talk to her about what was going on at the office.

It had been nice to feel useful to the family business again that way. The idea of spending more time doing just that—of it being her actual job—made her glow a little inside. If things carried on going this well, Frankie could have two parents who loved and made time for him, she could have a career she enjoyed and that fulfilled her, and she could even have a partnership with a husband who respected her, and who she respected in return.

Not a bad life, by anyone's standards.

But will it be enough?

Maria shook the thought away as she realised that Seb wasn't leading them towards the town of Mont Coeur. Instead, they'd swerved off the main road and were tramping through a field towards...

'We're going ice-skating?' she asked, her voice high with excitement as she spotted the frozen lake before them.

When had she last been out on the ice? She tried to remember as Seb pulled two pairs of skates from his bag and presented one to her with a flourish. She must have skated since that night with Seb fifteen years ago, surely? But if she had, she couldn't remember it.

Whenever she thought of ice-skating, she thought of him, and remembered that night.

'Think you remember how?' Seb asked, as he laced up his own skates, perching on a low fence to do so. 'Or have you secretly been keeping up your training when I wasn't looking?'

Maria shook her head. 'No training.' There was no rink near her parents' estate, and the lake froze only rarely—plus, without Seb to sneak out with her, what was the point? The only place she'd have ever skated would be Mont Coeur, and the Cattaneos tended more towards skiing than skating, so she had, too.

'Me neither.' Seb held out a hand to pull her up from the fence, so they could totter towards the ice together. 'But if we hold hands, I'm sure we'll be fine.'

'Hold my hand. I'll keep you safe.'

As his fingers wrapped around hers, she could almost hear seventeen-year-old Seb saying the words, as he had that night.

Just like then, she clung on tight as they took their first steps onto the ice. But this time she wasn't holding on for fear of the ice breaking— this lake was so shallow it froze hard all winter— or of her parents catching them. This time she just didn't ever want to let go.

'Ready?' Seb asked. Maria nodded.

And then…oh, then they were flying. The cold night air stung her cheeks as they spun around in wide circles on the ice, whipping past the snow-covered trees and the silent mountains beyond. For the first time in so long, Maria felt *free*. Leaving Seb hadn't brought her that freedom she'd sought so desperately, but *he* had, just for this one night.

As she gripped Seb's hand, it was as if the whole world fell away, until all that mattered was them and this perfect moment.

Just as it had the night she'd fallen in love with him, all those years before.

Maria let out a whoop of joy as Seb spun her, and his echoing laugh filled the whole sky.

Eventually, out of breath and still laughing, they fell down onto the snow beside the lake, hands still clutched together.

'Feel better for that?' Seb asked, and Maria nodded, unable to find the words. 'Good.' Releasing her fingers, he wrapped his arms around her, pulling her up between his legs so she could rest her back against his chest. 'Me, too. Much better than contracts.'

Maria laughed. 'I never thought I'd hear you say that.'

'I should have. Spending time with you… that's always been better than any business deal or meeting could be.'

Something tightened in her chest at his words. 'I'm happy to hear that.' Did he really mean it? Because if he did…it wasn't a declaration of love, of course. But for Seb, it was pretty close.

'Can I ask you something?' Seb said, after a moment.

Maria turned her face so her cheek lay against his chest, and listened to his heartbeat. 'Of course.'

'Why did you marry me?'

It was the perfect night. Him, his wife, the moonlight and the ice. He could feel Maria's warmth pressed against him until it drowned out the chill of the snow beneath them as she relaxed in his arms.

Everything was just as it should be. Until he ruined it, like always.

'Why did you marry me?'

Maria jerked away, sitting up and turning to face him. 'What do you mean? You know why.'

Oh, well. In for a penny and all that.

Seb shook his head. 'No. I know why your father ordered you to marry me. What I don't know is why on earth you said yes.'

She could have had any man in the world. She was beautiful, intelligent, and so far out of his league that Seb hadn't believed his father the first time he'd told him the engagement had been arranged.

He'd always wondered what her father had done to force her into it—especially after she'd left him. But he'd never had the courage to ask.

Until now.

Maria stared straight into his eyes for a long moment, and Seb held her gaze. He could wait her out.

They'd laid so much about their relationship bare already, but how could they keep moving forward without unpeeling this last, vital layer?

Finally, Maria broke away, her gaze skittering off towards the mountains, and whatever lay beyond them.

'My father… I was away at university. You knew that, right?' Her voice was soft, tentative, and she paused for Seb to nod an acknowledgement before she continued. 'I was studying for a business degree, of course, and I had almost finished my second year when, one day, he showed up on the campus with no warning. I thought he must have a meeting locally or something. Thought it was nice of him to surprise me like that.

'He took me out for lunch at the fanciest restaurant in town, just like he always would. You know my father—he likes things because they're expensive, not because they're good. But then, as I was sitting there eating my overpriced starter, drinking one-hundred-euros-a-bottle wine, he said, "The company's going under. We either have to declare bankruptcy or you need to marry Sebastian Cattaneo."'

Instinctively, Seb reached out to hold her close again, silently cursing Antonio Rossi as he did so. He'd always known the old man was a bastard, but he'd at least hoped he loved his daughter.

Apparently not so much.

Maria nestled back into his arms like she belonged there, and Seb allowed himself a moment of satisfaction before she continued her story.

'I argued that there had to be another way. I wanted to look at the books, talk to the investors, figure out a way to save the company using everything I'd learned about business. But he wouldn't even let me try.'

'You never told me,' Seb whispered, hating that she'd been so desperate not to marry him, and forced into it anyway. 'When I proposed…you smiled. You said it was what you wanted.'

'And you gave me an out.' Maria looked up at him, her eyes wide and serious. 'You told me that if I didn't want to marry you, I just had to say the word and you'd find another way.'

'But you didn't,' Seb replied. 'You said yes. Why?'

Maria sighed, and looked away. 'Because…because it was the best solution. If my father wasn't going to let me be of any use to his company, better we merge with yours and I have a chance to make a difference there instead. Marrying you… it meant I escaped that mausoleum my parents called home. Meant I could stay a part of the Cattaneo family for ever, instead of just on visits in the holidays. And you and I…we were friends, always. I figured there were a lot of things worse than marrying you.'

Hardly a ringing endorsement, Seb noted. But all those things she'd wanted from the marriage, he could still give her. His parents were gone, but the Cattaneos were still very much a family. And they'd already proved they were a great business team that afternoon. As for friends… He hoped they could be much more than that. But if friends was all he got, he'd take it.

A horrible thought occurred to him. One he'd had before, but had never realised the depth of before.

'I can't imagine how bad life with me must have been, then, to send you back to your parents.' The words came out choked, and Maria turned to kneel up in front of him, her cold palm pressed against his cheek. He gazed down into her dark blue eyes, shaded in the night, and realised a truth that had eluded him for far too long. Or perhaps he'd just never thought to look for it.

This woman is everything.

He had to make her happy. Had to give her the life she deserved. Had to be the *husband* she deserved, and the father that Frankie did, too.

Somehow. He'd figure it out.

Because nothing else mattered.

'It's getting better,' Maria whispered.

Then she kissed him, soft and sweet and perfect.

And suddenly Sebastian Cattaneo had hope again.

'Papà!' Frankie came flying into Sebastian's office a few days later, waving a sheet of shiny paper in his hand. His eyes were bright with excitement, and he bounced on his toes even when he came to a stop. 'Look, Papà!'

Noemi followed close behind, smiling indulgently and giving Seb the distinct impression that whatever happened next was going to be his sister's fault. Like so many other things in their childhood, actually. And this week.

Unbidden, Seb's mind flashed back to ice-skating with Maria, and the feel of her lips against his again after so long. They'd been giggling as they'd raced back to the chalet, hand in hand, ice skates clanking in the bag on his shoulder. He'd hoped—oh, how he'd hoped—that they'd have a chance to follow up their new-found closeness when they got home. Noemi and Max would have finished reading Frankie stories by then, and he should be fast asleep.

Except when they'd arrived, they'd found every light in the chalet blazing and Frankie jumping around the Christmas tree on a sugar high of excitement, amplified by an afternoon at the toy store.

Maria had dropped his hand before they were even through the door. And since then there hadn't been a moment when he'd felt the same closeness, or the same sense of possibility.

He had to find a way to get back there. And soon—because Christmas was nearly upon them.

They'd all managed nearly a week of harmony

at the Mont Coeur chalet now, and things were starting to feel more relaxed, more natural, at least. He and Maria were both still keeping up their respective sides of the bargain, and Frankie was luxuriating in all the attention from his parents. Leo and Anissa had stopped in to see them almost every day, and there had been plenty of family dinners and conversations—enough to make Seb feel that just maybe they could be a real family, even after everything.

It probably didn't hurt that the Christmas spirit had infused the place so completely that even Seb was dreaming of cinnamon and pine needles.

Well, actually, that wasn't true. He was dreaming about Maria, and that kiss. Every single night, as she slept in the next room with Frankie. Without him.

But he was feeling festive, which was a whole lot more than he'd managed this time last year. And so was everyone else, it seemed. The Mont Coeur chalet was a haven of good cheer and amicability for the first time in what felt like an age.

And Frankie had come to find him, of his own accord, because he wanted to see him. What more could he ask for?

Mindful of his agreement with Maria, Seb shut his laptop, hoping that the emails he'd only just started to deal with could wait a little longer, and gave Frankie his full attention.

'What have you got there?' he asked, lifting the little boy up into his lap.

Frankie shoved the shiny paper towards Seb's nose, and Noemi snorted with laughter as he tried to prise it from his son's tiny fist.

The paper was red, gold and green—and glittery. Clearly no expense had been spared in the preparation of this flyer.

'Santa's coming!' Frankie cried, even as Seb read the words confirming that the man in red was indeed visiting Mont Coeur on the day before Christmas Eve—two days' time. Perfect.

'Will you take me to meet *Babbo Natale*, Papà?' Frankie asked sweetly, using the Italian name for Santa, and Seb couldn't help but smile at the excitement in his eyes.

'Of course I will.'

Frankie bounced himself right off Seb's lap in the resulting joy and celebration, after giving his *papà* as giant a hug as little two-year-old arms could manage. Then he bounded back towards the door to hug Noemi, and promptly crashed into his mother coming the other way.

'Mamma! Papà's going to take me to see Santa!'

Maria raised her eyebrows as she looked across the chalet's office at Seb. He waved the garish flyer in explanation. 'He wants to go.'

'Of course he does.' Maria's mouth twitched in what Seb suspected was an effort to keep from grinning. 'Are you hoping you've been a good enough boy to ask for a treat this Christmas, too?'

Heat filled his body just at the flirtatious tone of her voice. God, he was so far gone with wanting her, it was insane. He didn't remember feeling like this ever before—except maybe on their wedding day, waiting to be alone with her, waiting for their life together to start.

'Do you think I stand a chance?' he asked baldly.

For the first time since their kiss, Maria didn't pull back at the suggestion. 'Do you know, I think you just might.'

Seb's heart soared. Finally, finally, it felt like he was getting somewhere.

At this point in a business negotiation he'd know exactly what to do next—push the advantage. But could he risk it with Maria? She *had* said theirs was a business partnership...

And she was already halfway out of the door with Frankie, Noemi following behind. If he wanted to act, it had to be now.

He stood up behind his desk. 'In that case, I think you owe me another date.'

Maria paused in the doorway and raised her eyebrows at him. 'I *owe* you?'

Noemi was shaking her head at him. He ignored her.

'That was part of our deal, yes? Regular catch-up meetings in romantic settings.' He was still kind of amazed he'd got that one past her. She'd been so determined to keep everything business-like, and he, well…hadn't been.

'I suppose I did agree to that.'

'Then tonight?' he pressed.

Maria shook her head. 'Noemi and Leo both have plans tonight, so no willing babysitter.'

Seb glanced over at his sister to check the truth of this statement.

'Sorry,' Noemi said unapologetically.

'Then we'll have the house to ourselves,' Seb said, glancing down to see Frankie still bouncing beside Maria. 'Well, us and Frankie. We'll have date night at home.'

'I…' Maria's mouth was open, but no more words were coming out.

'Dinner at eight,' Seb said. 'I'm cooking.'

That was how you won a negotiation.

CHAPTER ELEVEN

MARIA SMOOTHED DOWN the soft jersey dress she'd chosen for the evening, and hoped against hope that Frankie wouldn't choose tonight to wake up with a bad dream, or wanting another cup of milk, or whatever. She'd finally settled him down—after three books about *Babbo Natale* and his reindeer, helpfully supplied by his aunt Noemi—while Seb was bashing about in the kitchen downstairs, and then realised that if this really was a date night, she should probably change out of the jeans and jumper she'd been wearing all day.

She hadn't exactly packed for parties or fancy nights out, but she had included a forest-green jersey dress, with a twist at the waist that made her slender curvy shape into a true hourglass, and a cowl neckline that dipped low enough to show off her best lingerie.

That she was only wearing because it went with the dress. Not because she expected Seb to be stripping it from her later.

Probably.

Oh, who was she kidding? That was *exactly* what she was expecting.

Since their trip to the lake, Maria had been

feeling the tension between them more than ever. Every smile Seb gave her, every look…she could feel the heat in it. Could remember the sensation of his lips under hers as she'd kissed him, his breath against her skin as she'd pulled away. The amazed look in his eyes. The way his hand at her waist had made her tremble…

And, of course, it had gone nowhere, because that was the reality of life with a toddler. But this time Frankie was asleep, the rest of the house was empty, and anything could happen. And maybe it just might.

In fact, making love with Seb tonight would be the perfect end to a pretty perfect week. Yes, Seb had still worked most days—he wouldn't be the driven and conscientious man she'd married if he hadn't—but he'd called on her to talk things through once or twice, and he'd always turned the laptop off in time for a family dinner. And he'd been surprisingly patient with Frankie's many, many interruptions during his office hours. Plus he'd actually taken whole afternoons off some days to play with Frankie in the snow, attempt more ski lessons, or just show him around Mont Coeur. They'd even managed to take him on a sleigh ride—although Frankie still wasn't sure about the huge horses that pulled the sleigh. Apparently he'd prefer reindeer, like Santa had.

In short, Seb had given her a picture-perfect view of what life could be like with him, if he stuck to their agreement.

Now it was her turn to keep to the contract.

A romantic date night. And maybe more… A shiver ran through Maria's body just at the thought.

With one last check on the sleeping Frankie, Maria headed down the stairs to the large, state-of-the-art kitchen. There was a formal dining room for special occasions—where Maria fully expected that they'd be eating Christmas dinner in just a few days—but tonight she found that Seb had laid the small table in the breakfast nook, with a delicate display of seasonal greenery in the middle, and a couple of low candles giving it a romantic air.

'I thought this was more…intimate than the dining room.' Seb handed her a glass of white wine, and bent to kiss her cheek. 'You look beautiful, by the way.'

That was another thing. Seb had made a point of telling her how beautiful she was at least once a day for the last week. As if he was making up for all the years when he'd barely seemed to see her at all.

It was almost enough to make her believe that this time it really could all be different.

'Is Frankie asleep?' Seb asked, returning to the

stove to stir whatever was in the pot that smelled so delicious.

Maria nodded. 'I think your ski lesson this afternoon wore him out. That and all the Santa excitement, courtesy of Noemi.'

Seb flashed her a smile. 'He did seem pretty excited about the idea of meeting *Babbo Natale*.'

'So did you,' Maria replied. She settled herself on a stool at the kitchen counter to watch him cook. 'This is the first year he's really understood about the concept of Santa—or even Christmas, really. So it's all new and exciting for him.'

'I can't tell you how glad I am that I get to share that with him,' Seb said.

Maria shifted uncomfortably on her stool, very aware that *she* was the reason that Seb had missed Frankie's second Christmas. They'd have to ensure that his third was a great one to make up for it.

'What are we eating?' she asked, eager to change the subject. Seb hadn't cooked for her very often—by the time he'd got home in the evenings it had usually been too late to start and, besides, Maria liked to cook. But she also knew that Nicole Cattaneo wouldn't let any child of hers out into the world without being able to cook some Italian classics.

Or knowing how to serve a perfect antipasti plate. Maria picked at the platter of cured meats, olives, roasted vegetables and cheeses, and felt her stomach rumble in anticipation. If nothing else about tonight went to plan, at least the food should be good.

'That pasta and sausage dish of Mamma's that you always loved,' Seb replied, stirring the sauce. 'Want to taste? Check it's as good as you remember?'

She nodded eagerly, and he lifted his spoon from the pan with a small sampling of sauce on the end, and held it over the counter for her to try. Maria blew to cool it, then let the delicious, spicy sauce luxuriate on her taste buds as her eyes fluttered closed.

'Okay?' Seb asked, a hint of nervousness in his voice.

'Perfect.' Maria opened her eyes to find him watching her intently. And, before she could even guess what he was about to do, Seb dropped his spoon to the counter and leaned across it, his tall frame allowing him to reach her easily.

Then he kissed her, and Maria forgot all about the taste of the pasta sauce, and let herself fall into the taste of him instead.

Oh, God, he'd forgotten how good this felt, even in the few days since he'd last kissed her. It was as if his mind couldn't believe the memory was as sensational as it truly was.

Seb cursed the counter between them, blocking his ability to sweep Maria into his arms and hold her close. But then, as they broke the kiss, coming apart just enough to breathe and stare at each other, Seb decided it might be for the best.

He'd wanted to romance her tonight. To show her how ready he was to be the kind of husband she needed—in every way. To focus on her completely.

If he took her to bed before they even got to dinner, he would kind of be missing the point.

So he pulled back, smiling at the sight of her flushed skin, bright eyes, and her chest heaving with too-fast breaths under that gorgeously slinky dress. He was just about to think of something wonderfully suave and seductive to say when the pasta boiled over behind him.

'Hold that thought,' he said, and turned to deal with the culinary crisis.

Ten minutes later, dinner was served.

'Is it like you remember?' he asked, as Maria tucked in. He was pretty sure he'd recalled his mother's recipe correctly, but not having her there to ask had brought him down for a few minutes, the way it always did when he remembered that they were gone.

But his parents would approve of his attempts to win Maria back, he was sure. Well, his father would be worrying about him neglecting the business, but Mamma would understand, and she'd talk his *papà* round. She always did.

'It's perfect,' Maria replied, smiling. 'Just as I remember. Your mother always made this for me the first night of my visits. Do you remember?'

'I do. In fact, I took it as evidence that you were always her secret favourite, long before you actually married into the family.'

Maria laughed. 'I think she just liked cooking for an appreciate audience. You and Noemi were too used to her incredible meals. My mother liked us to pretend we could exist on air and water alone. I used to long to escape her steamed chicken and salads and come to your place for proper food.'

'I knew there had to be something that kept you hanging around us,' Seb replied. 'I was just hoping it had a little bit more to do with my charm and good looks.'

'Oh, there was definitely that appeal, too,' Maria said, with another flirtatious smile. 'But mostly...mostly I just liked the way your family felt like, well, a *real* family. Mine was always more like three people stuck together because they had nowhere else to go.'

Seb remembered how she'd spoken about escaping her parents' home by marrying him. Which led to the memory of the first Christmas they were married, and how they'd spent it in the chilly atmosphere of the Rossi mansion. He knew exactly what she meant. There was a reason they'd agreed to always spend Christmas with Sebastian's family after that.

'Do they mind you being here for Christmas with Frankie this year?' he asked, aware that it was rather late to be asking that question. If they did, it wouldn't have stopped him asking her to come to Mont Coeur anyway. But Maria had been living with them for a full year…

'I didn't tell them,' Maria admitted, topping up her wine glass.

Seb blinked. 'You don't think they might notice you're gone? I mean, Frankie kind of fills a place with sound. If nothing else, they might remark on the sudden quiet.'

'They're away visiting with friends for the holidays. Besides, I wasn't *exactly* staying with them,' Maria said. 'I mean, the idea was to find somewhere Frankie and I could be happier. And that place was never going to be with my parents.'

That stung a little, but Seb acknowledged the truth of it. Though he felt slightly reassured that even being married to him was, in fact, better than staying with her parents. 'So where have you been living?'

'Do you remember the little cottage on the edge of their estate? Down by the lake?'

'The one we ice-skated on? Of course. I remember escaping to that cottage the first Christmas Eve we were married, and spending the evening together away from them. It was…very cosy.' It had been tiny, even by normal house standards, and Maria was used to mansions and luxury chalets. Beyond its size, the only thing Seb could really remember about it was how he'd made love to Maria in front of the fire…

'I love it there,' Maria said, breaking into his memories. 'And Frankie does, too. He spent time with my parents—well, mostly my mother—but I think we both liked having somewhere that was just ours to go home to.'

'You liked it being just the two of you?' Seb asked, his heart sinking a little. That was something he definitely couldn't give her.

'It made Frankie and me closer than we might have been otherwise,' Maria said. 'But in lots of ways it didn't feel all that much different from living with you.' She gave him a tiny apologetic smile as she spoke, but it did nothing to ease the guilt and pain eating him up inside.

Seb laid his fork on his almost empty bowl, his appetite gone. 'And now? Have you felt that this week?' *It's getting better*, she'd told him. He had to hope that was enough.

Because if she said yes, it was game over, nowhere else to go. He'd done his best—within realistic boundaries. He couldn't give up his business completely. That would never work long term. But he'd thrown himself into finding a balance that kept everyone happy.

Had it been enough?

Maria placed her fork down, too, pushing her bowl away and meeting his gaze as the candles guttered and flickered, down to the end of their wicks. 'This week…this week has felt like something completely new between us. Something I like very much.'

'I'm glad.' Relief flooded through him at her words. 'And I feel the same. In fact, I'm hoping it might continue for a very long time.'

'I hope so, too.' Maria held his gaze so long that Seb could feel heat rising in him just from the way she looked at him. Like she was seeing him anew. Like she wanted what she saw.

In which case…

'How do you feel about taking dessert upstairs?' he suggested, the final part of his plan for the evening falling nicely into place.

'To the living room?' Maria asked.

Seb shook his head. 'I was thinking the hot tub.'

The hot tub wasn't exactly the ideal place to eat tiramisu, but Maria was past caring. This wasn't about pudding anyway. This was about them.

Being husband and wife again.

While Seb transferred their dessert into something easier to eat from than the large dish he'd bought it in, Maria slipped into the bedroom she shared with Frankie and tried to dig out her swimming costume quietly. She really, *really* didn't want to wake her little boy up right now. She wanted to get changed quickly and get back out there to her husband.

Unless she didn't bother with the swimming costume part. If Seb showed up to find her naked in the hot tub, he'd definitely know he'd been good enough to make the nice list, right? No need to check it twice or anything.

After a week and a half of both of them trying to live up to the other's expectations, Maria was more than ready to say enough and just jump back into bed with her husband. Or hot tub. Wherever, to be honest. She just wanted her marriage back— new and improved, but still *her* marriage. The one she'd thought she could never have again.

With her husband. The one she loved.

That thought stopped her cold, and she held her swimming costume to her chest as she realised. She'd got so carried away with how well things were going, she hadn't even noticed that the word 'love' still wasn't on Sebastian's lips. He'd embraced the whole business partnership marriage idea—even if he had his own ideas about how much romance that might entail—and he'd been living up to the goals and objectives she'd set for him, just like he would at work.

What if she was just another job? What if he just wanted to tick 'Win back wife' off his goals-for-the-year list?

What if that was still all she was to him—another acquisition? One he had fun with, slept with, even talked and worked with—but still just another part of the Cattaneo treasury, at the end of the day.

She bit her lip, and scrunched the costume up in her hands. Did it really matter, anyway? If he never said *I love you*—if he never even felt it. As long as he kept behaving the way she wanted him to—with respect and affection for her and their family—wasn't that enough?

She could live with that. Especially if it meant she got to have sex with the most gorgeous man she'd ever met in a hot tub tonight.

Before she could change her mind, she changed quickly out of her dress and into her swimming costume, wrapping her dressing gown around her for added warmth. The chalet itself might have superb central heating, but the hot tub...the hot tub was out on the balcony. In the snow.

At least the water would be warm. And maybe the chill in the air would help her cool her over-heated mind. And libido, come to that.

She stepped out of the room to find Seb already

out on the balcony, two pots of tiramisu balanced on the edge of the hot tub as he finished running the water. She frowned. She knew from past experience that the tub took at least a couple of hours to fill and heat properly. Which meant he had to have been planning this from the start.

Sneaky.

But to be honest, she couldn't really blame him. If he was feeling half as frustrated by their lack of a physical relationship as she was, she was kind of surprised he hadn't just pulled her into the bathtub because it was quicker.

And it meant he was thinking ahead *about them*. The same as with dinner—digging out her favourite recipe, her favourite wine, buying the food and making it… He was making an effort. A real, sustained effort.

And wasn't that exactly what she'd asked for, really?

Didn't he deserve the same in return?

Ducking back into the shadows, Maria watched Seb for a moment as he fiddled with the tub, until she was certain he hadn't spotted she was there. Then she shimmied out of her costume under her robe, left it hanging off the back of the sofa and strode out onto the balcony to meet her husband.

Seb turned and smiled as she closed the door behind her. 'Ready?' he asked.

'Definitely,' Maria said.

Then she dropped the robe and watched Seb's eyes widen.

The look on his face had made the risk of hypothermia totally worth it, Maria decided later. As she stretched out under the luxury sheets on Sebastian's bed, watching his chest rise and fall as he slept beside her, she knew without a doubt she had made the right decision. Maybe he never would love her the way she loved him, but the new man she'd come home to had made up for not saying the words with the quality of his actions. Respect and adoration could be every bit as wonderful as that fabled true love nonsense, she'd decided.

Especially when he could make her body sing the way he had tonight. Every inch of her still tingled with the memory. She'd half thought, over the last year, that she must have imagined how phenomenal they were, moving together in sync, their bodies as one. But if anything, it had been even better than she remembered from their honeymoon.

A perfect moment.

It might be her very own Christmas miracle. Her husband really saw her at last—and she truly believed that they could be happy together, as a family.

Maria was still smiling as she fell asleep.

But when she woke up alone, a handful of hours later, it was a very different story.

CHAPTER TWELVE

SEB HAD HAD plans for this morning. Important plans that involved waking up before his son and persuading his wife to relive their hot tub activities from the night before. Just in case he'd only dreamed how amazing it had been. He hadn't, he knew. No dream he'd ever experienced had been *that* vivid or *that* incredible.

From the moment she'd dropped that silky dressing gown, and he'd seen her perfect body again, skin glowing with the moonlight reflecting off the snow, he'd known that his Christmas was complete. Taking her into the water with him, holding her in his arms again, moving with her as they'd found their pleasure together... It had been the confirmation he'd needed that everything they'd been working towards had been possible.

She was his wife again. She trusted him with her body again, and her happiness. She would stay now; he knew it. Not because of the amazing sex but because of what it had meant for her to stand there naked on the balcony before him.

Trust. Partnership. That was what they'd wanted, and that was what they'd found again.

Maybe that partnership contract idea hadn't

been so stupid after all. And he'd been looking forward to thanking Maria for coming up with it—in a rather intimate, physical way—that morning.

But instead he found himself on a private helicopter, speeding towards Geneva to deal with a last-minute crisis with the Swiss merger.

The Italian arm of the business never had this sort of problem the day before Christmas Eve, he thought mulishly.

He hadn't wanted to go. But he simply hadn't had any other choice.

When his phone had buzzed just before five a.m. that morning, his first instinct had been to ignore it. Maria, deeply asleep beside him, hadn't seemed to be bothered by it. And when he'd planned to wake up before Frankie did, he hadn't meant quite *that* early.

But then it had buzzed again, and Maria had shifted in her sleep, giving a small moan, and he'd known he had to answer it before it woke her.

Of course, then he'd seen the screen, and the panicked text messages from his deputy, on duty in Geneva, and he'd known that this wasn't going to be anything approaching a good day.

The contract he and Maria had spent hours picking apart, the one she'd helped him make sense of—the last deal his father had ever worked on—was about to implode. And he was the only person who could stop it. So, gathering up all the notes he and Maria had made, he'd kissed her sleeping forehead, and left.

The worst part—after leaving Maria—had been having to ride in a damn helicopter.

He'd taken this trip half a dozen times before, and travelled by helicopter transfer to the Mont Coeur chalet more times than he cared to remember. But that had been before his parents had died in a helicopter crash.

He hadn't had too much time to think about it, to start with. At first, he'd just been concentrating on not waking Maria as he'd dressed, then on making sure he had all the relevant documents with him to try to salvage an almost impossible situation. This deal was only the first in a series that was supposed to secure the future of the company beyond the Italian borders. If it went south, his shares might not even be worth the paperwork it would take to sign them over.

His father had wanted a big gesture, something to show that his work was done, and Seb was ready to take over the company fully. And he'd found it—a huge expansion into new territories. He'd been so sure it was all tied up, every t crossed and every i dotted. And Seb had known that even if his father hadn't lived to see it, Salvo Cattaneo's legacy would live on through the company, getting bigger and brighter every year.

Until this morning, and a last-minute contract issue that could blow the whole thing. Worst of all, it was one that Maria had pointed out to him when they'd worked on the contract—one that he'd assured her would be fine.

It wasn't anywhere close to fine, as it turned out.

He'd screwed up again. He'd put his father's last-ever deal at risk. The whole *company* at risk. His father's legacy hung on him getting this right.

And he could never let his father down.

So here he was, sitting aboard a precarious flying machine with whirring blades that made him see his parents' terrified faces every time they rotated, preparing to fix it. Perfect way to spend the day before Christmas Eve, really.

Closing his eyes, Seb focused on Maria's face in his mind. The gleam in her eyes as she'd dropped that robe and stepped into the hot tub, stark naked. The way she'd insisted on eating tiramisu—also naked—before she'd even let him kiss her. The way she'd melted in his arms when they'd finally, finally touched...

The helicopter banked sharply to the right, and Seb clung to the base of his seat with white knuckles, his heart racing with fear.

All he had to do was get through this helicopter ride, the meeting from hell, and then one more

trip back home to Mont Coeur. Then he was taking Christmas Eve off, come hell or high water.
He'd fix the contract, pick up a bottle of cham-
pagne on his way back to the helipad, and then
he'd go home to Maria and Frankie and enjoy
Christmas, in a way he'd never hoped to again.

He just had to make it through this. Then everything would be wonderful again.

How could it not be, now he had Maria back
home where she belonged?

'What do you mean, he left?' Noemi's beautiful brows crumpled up in a confused frown.
'It's the day before Christmas Eve. We all had
plans. With Frankie. And You Know Who.' She
mouthed 'Santa' in a deliberate manner in case
Maria hadn't picked up on the inference.

She had. And even if she hadn't, how could
she have forgotten the promised Santa trip, with
Frankie reminding her every moment since he'd
woken up?

Although Seb seemed to have managed it.
Probably because he hadn't been there when
Maria and Frankie had woken up.

Wordlessly, Maria handed Noemi the note Seb
had left stuck to the bedside table for her to find
that morning. Noemi scanned the sticky note, her
eyes widening. Then she went back to the beginning and read it out loud.

'*"Had to fly to Geneva—work stuff. Hope to be back for dinner. S. x."* Well, that's…succinct.'

'Exactly.' So much for all those promises to involve her in his world—the business as well as the personal. Apparently it all fell by the wayside the moment some more interesting 'work stuff' appeared.

All of it, including their son.

Frankie sat on the stairs in the hallway, holding his toy fox close to his chest and looking more forlorn than Maria thought she'd ever seen a toddler look. He'd been so excited about today—about seeing Santa, of course, but Maria knew the real appeal had been taking his *papà* to see Santa.

And stupid Papà was in stupid Geneva.

'He said he flew…' Noemi's face was strangely pale, and it took Maria a moment or two to connect the dots and figure out why.

'He'll have taken a helicopter,' she said faintly. Of course he would have. It was the obvious and fastest mode of transport from Mont Coeur to Geneva, and one he'd taken numerous times before when he'd been setting up the Swiss office.

But that had been before. Before Salvo and Nicole had died flying in one in New York, where they were supposed to be meeting Leo. Maria's heart pounded against her ribs at the thought of Seb so desperate to get back to work that he'd willingly climb into one again and fly away from them all the day before Christmas Eve. *How could he?*

'Have you called him?' Noemi asked. Maria could tell what her friend was really asking. *Do you think he's okay?*

'Not yet.' How could she? He'd made his choices very clear once again. Work before family, business before his wife. Just like always.

The worst part was that she'd honestly believed he'd changed. She'd thought that he'd finally seen the value of their marriage, the importance of their son. She'd thought they had a future.

Apparently Seb had simply wanted to get her into bed again, and now that mission was accomplished and he felt secure that she'd be moving home, he could get back to what he *actually* cared about most in the world. Work.

Well, at least she knew the truth now rather than later. If this had happened after their agreed trial period, once she'd already moved back in with him, had told Frankie they were staying with Papà for good…that would have been much worse. Small mercies and silver linings, she supposed. Her heart might be breaking again, but at least it was something that she found out now—before she got Frankie's hopes up. Or hers.

Seb might never have learned that lesson about

counting chickens before they were hatched, but that was working to her advantage right now. And he never had been a patient man. She shouldn't really be surprised.

Unbidden, memories of their last fight, the night before she'd left, just over a year before, came back to haunt her...

'Where were you?' she'd yelled, the moment he'd breezed through the door. 'You promised you'd be here.'

'I got caught up at work.'

Seb had looked surprised she'd even noticed.

'There was a problem with one of the new campaigns, took for ever to straighten out. Does it matter?'

'Yes, it matters!'

How could she ever make him understand? she'd thought.

'You haven't even seen your son in three days. That *matters*, Seb.'

'Look, work's been crazy. Trust me, I'd rather have been here. I'm exhausted. I'll make it up to Frankie at the weekend,' he'd promised.

And she had even believed that he'd meant it.

Except he'd promised the same thing every weekend for a month.

And then she'd known. It would never happen.

She'd shaken her head. 'I don't believe you.'

With a groan, Seb had dropped his briefcase

to the floor. 'Come on, Maria. You knew what you were signing up for. You married me to save your family business—just like I married you to get the merger between our companies. And now you're complaining that I'm spending too much time working at that same business?'

She'd stumbled back a few steps. She'd dared to hope that their marriage was something more, and in just a few words he'd proved that it was even less than she'd thought.

She was nothing to him.

And he was everything to her.

'You don't even *see* me!' she'd yelled. 'Sometimes I'm not sure you'd even notice if I left.'

'You're making this into something this isn't, Maria…'

But she hadn't been. For the first time she'd seen their marriage clearly.

Suddenly calm, she had forced herself to stand up straight, to look him in the eye and accept the truth.

'This isn't enough for me, Seb. And I realise now that you can't give me what I need. You're not capable of it.'

She'd known it then. And now it was happening all over again.

Time to face the truth.

'I need to pack,' Maria said, and Frankie suddenly looked up at her, his eyes wide. Maria tried to look calm and happy for his sake—she could never tell how much he understood in his little two-year-old mind. Some days the very concept of time and place seemed beyond him. Others… he seemed to understand the world around them better than she did.

'You're leaving?' Noemi asked, and Maria gave a helpless shrug.

'How can I stay?' She'd asked for what she needed to be happy. A family. A commitment from him to be a real part of that family.

And he'd flown off to Geneva instead of taking Frankie to meet Santa.

That was her answer, right there.

And she'd set *terms*, damn it. They had a *contract*. How could she hold her head up high again if she let him break it now? He'd know that he could break it again and again in the future with no repercussions.

That was no way to do business. And she was a businesswoman now.

'I want to see Santa,' Frankie said suddenly, standing up on the bottom step. 'I want to see Santa *now*.'

Maria was about to give her usual lecture about asking politely, even though she didn't really have the energy, but Noemi got there first.

'Of course we'll go and see Santa, my cherub!' She wrapped her arms around Frankie's thin shoulders and held him and his fox close. 'We'll go and see him together right now. Frankie and Mamma and Aunt Noemi.'

'No!' Frankie wriggled free. 'I want to go with Papà!'

Maria sighed. Of course he did. That was what he'd been promised. And while he might forget how to brush his teeth or to say 'please' and 'thank you', Frankie never forgot a promise. Something Seb would know if he'd been paying proper attention.

'Papà's not here, *piccolo*,' she said, as gently as she could.

Not gently enough, apparently.

Frankie flew into a frenzy of sobbing, throwing himself face down on the stairs and burying his face in his hands. 'I want Papà! Papà!' he cried, and Maria's heart broke a little bit more.

Noemi looked at her with panic in her eyes. 'What shall I do? How do we fix it?'

Because she didn't know that only Sebastian could do that—and he didn't seem to want to.

'We can't,' Maria said. 'All we can do is ride it out.'

Noemi winced as Frankie gave a particularly ear-splitting wail. 'How? With earplugs?'

Maria shook her head. 'You go and get Max, and buy more ice cream. I'll deal with this. Then when he's calmer he can have ice cream with you two while I pack. It'll be a nice last memory before we leave.'

Noemi looked like she wanted to argue, but Maria kept her expression set and, after a second or two, Noemi nodded and headed towards the kitchen.

And Maria sank down onto the stairs, drew her son into her arms and pretended she wasn't crying as she whispered reassurances in his ear.

It was dark by the time the helicopter blades whirred to a stop on the Mont Coeur helipad. With a weary sigh, Seb gathered his belongings, thanked the pilot and headed back to the chalet in search of a stiff drink—and his wife.

He smiled to himself at the realisation. However awful today had been—and it had been pretty bloody terrible—he was still excited to go home and talk to Maria about it. She'd understand about how terrified he'd been of the helicopter ride. And she'd sympathise with the ridiculous contract screw-up that had dragged him out there to renegotiate at the eleventh hour with their new partners, just to ensure the family business didn't lose millions further down the line—even if she did tell him that she'd told him so.

She'd understand. She'd pour him a drink, listen, then kiss all his cares away.

This was why he needed his wife back.

A year ago, he'd never imagined they could get back here. A year ago, he had still been replaying that last argument over and over in his head, trying to make sense of it.

He'd been so exhausted at the time he hadn't even been sure he remembered it right. It had just made no sense. Yes, he'd been late home and, yes, it hadn't been the first time. But he'd never understood what had made that time different.

He'd apologised, as always. And when she'd thrown it back at him, he'd reminded her of the truth.

This was why she'd married him. For his company. For him to work hard, to build a new family business for them—and for Frankie. He was working *for* his son.

Just like his *papà* had worked for him and Noemi. If he could do half the job his *papà* had, Frankie would be okay.

It was just that being even half the man Salvo Cattaneo had been, living up to that impossible ideal, took time and energy—and it didn't leave a lot left over.

That was something Maria *hadn't* understood.

But now, finally, they seemed to be understanding each other at last. Now he was on the way to being the husband she needed.

When he finally reached the chalet, most of the windows were already dark. He checked his watch—it was later than he'd thought. God, this day had gone on for ever.

Then he frowned. The one light that still shone out into the night came from a room on the second floor, to the right...yes. It was his office window. Why was that room lit?

Letting himself in, he headed straight up to investigate. He had a bottle of whisky in the drawer there anyway—a result of reading too many bad detective novels as a child, Maria had always said—and there was no point turning on all the other lights in the large chalet just for a drink. He could de-stress just as well in his office, then head to bed and see if Maria was feeling amenable to being woken up.

Then he opened his office door and found his wife sitting in his chair, drinking his whisky, her feet resting on the desk beside a familiar green, red and glittery flyer.

Santa. Frankie. That was today.

Seb stalled in the doorway, leaning heavily against the frame. *Oh, God.* 'Maria, I—'

'I don't care,' she snapped. She swung her legs down from the desk and pushed herself to a standing position, resting her hands on either side of that flyer as she leaned forward. 'You promised to take your son to see Santa. And obviously that means very little to you, but it meant everything to him. He wouldn't go without you, you realise?

So he's just been miserable here all day, despite all the ice cream Noemi and Max have fed him. And then he cried himself to sleep when you still weren't back from your oh-so-important business trip.'

'It *was* important.' Seb sighed, running a hand over his hair as he tried to find a way to salvage this. He'd spent all day negotiating with idiots, and now he had to come home and do the same thing with his wife.

This was not how he'd imagined this evening going.

God, it was happening all over again. Just like last time, he was exhausted and strung out and nothing made any *sense*.

'*Frankie* is important, too.' Maria stared at him, as if she were waiting for a magical response that would make all things better. But he didn't have one.

Finally, she shook her head and straightened up. 'Look, I'm already packed. We couldn't get a flight out today or we'd be gone already, but we're booked on one at lunchtime tomorrow.'

Wait. What?

'You're leaving? You can't! You…you said you'd stay for Christmas.'

'And you said you'd put your family first for once over the holidays. You said you'd prove that if I stayed, things would be different.'

'And they *have* been different!' She'd admitted that herself last night. She couldn't take that back now, could she?

'Right up until the point where you got me into bed, yes.' Maria's expression turned hard. 'Was that what it was all about, in the end? You just wanted to prove you could have me again, and once you'd achieved that you didn't need to try any more?'

'No!' How could she think that? Well, apart from the bit where he'd slept with her then run out on her and his obligations the next morning.

How could he have been so stupid?

'It was the contract, Maria. Remember the clause you found—'

'Look, it doesn't matter now.' Maria cut him off, and sighed. 'We tried, Seb. We really did. But I'm never going to be happy being left behind while you chase after the adrenaline high of doing business. And neither is Frankie. I thought…'

'What? What did you think?' Because suddenly Seb had the sinking suspicion that he'd been misunderstanding her from the first. That all this talk of partnerships and contracts had been hiding something else. And if he didn't know what that was, how could he fix it?

'You can't give me what I need. You're not capable of it.'

He'd given her everything. Why wasn't it enough?

What wasn't she asking for?

'I thought it could be enough. If you could live by my rules, follow the plan…if we could make all that work, I thought a business partnership marriage would be enough.' Maria looked up and met his gaze, her eyes so open and honest that he knew that, finally, they were getting to the real reason she'd left him. Yes, he'd been a lousy husband and a workaholic, and he'd forgotten important things like anniversaries and birthdays and Santa. But she'd known that and had married him anyway. She'd known that and had come back anyway, ready to give him a second chance.

So why was this time different?

'But I know now I was wrong. Yes, you messed up today. But that's not why I'm leaving.' Maria took a deep breath. 'I'm leaving because even if you met every objective I set, it still wouldn't be enough.'

There was something more, he was sure.

'Enough for what?' he asked, his voice soft. He had to *listen*. He had to *understand*.

'Enough to make up for the fact that you were never going to love me the way I'd fallen in love with you.'

CHAPTER THIRTEEN

WELL, THERE IT WAS. She'd done it now. He'd probably be grateful she was leaving. He'd wanted a business wife, one who knew the terms of the deal—entertaining clients, bringing up his heir, and basically reliving her own mother's miserable life for the next fifty years. But he'd compromised—he'd offered her a job in the company, allowed her to have a say in what *she* needed, agreed to everything she'd asked for.

And it still wasn't enough.

Because she'd never been able to bring herself to ask for what she *really* wanted—until now. Maybe she was to blame, at least a little bit, for everything that had happened between them before. She'd never been honest about what she needed.

But now she was.

She'd been furious when she'd woken alone, and had realised that Seb had skipped out on their plans and let Frankie down. But if she was honest with herself, she knew that wasn't why she was leaving.

She was leaving because, if he loved her, she wouldn't need a contract or objectives or any of the other tactics she'd used to turn him into the husband she wanted.

If he loved her, he'd have woken her up and explained, and they'd have worked it out together. She could have even gone with him and held his hand on that awful helicopter for moral support if he'd needed it. But it hadn't even occurred to him to ask.

'You…'

'Fell in love with you. Yes. Before we were even married, probably. Definitely, actually.' She may as well own her truth now it was out there. 'Seb, I've loved you since I was fifteen—since the night you sneaked me out to go ice-skating. And then I fell in love with you all over again when we got married. And since I've been back…that feeling has only grown stronger, if I'm honest.'

'Then why are you leaving? If you love me, why do you have to go?' Maria could hear the frustration and confusion in Seb's voice. Of course he didn't understand. This wasn't the deal they'd struck. And Seb only understood negotiations and deals.

They couldn't negotiate love, though.

'Because you don't love me.' It was that simple and that impossible, all at the same time.

'Of course I love you!' Seb objected.

Maria shook her head. 'Okay, I know you love

me as a friend and partner. But you're not *in* love with me. You never have been.'

'I don't see what the difference is,' Seb said tiredly. 'Of course I love you, and Frankie. You're my wife. It's kind of part of the deal.' As if it were automatic, a foregone conclusion.

'That's the thing, Seb. It isn't.' Maria sighed. 'Think of it this way. When we got married, I was a business asset. And when we discovered that we actually got along and connected, well, physically, that was an added bonus, right? Then Frankie came along and you figured the job was done. You had the wife to support you and entertain clients, and you had an heir to take over the business when you were ready to retire. Right?'

Seb's uncomfortable expression told her that she'd got it *exactly* right.

'But that's not enough for me,' she said.

'I get that!' Seb exploded. 'That's why I've been jumping through hoops for the last week and a half to meet all your objectives! To give you what you want. You can have the job—hell, you can have the whole company if you want. After today, I'm not sure I'd miss it. But it's still not enough for you.'

'No,' Maria said simply. 'It isn't. Because the way I love you, Seb…it has nothing to do with business, or obligations, or expectations. It's not even about Frankie, really. It's just…all consuming. Like you're the first thing I think about in the morning and the last thing I dream about at night. Even when I was away, when I had to make a decision or wanted to try something, *you* were the person I wanted to talk to about it. But I couldn't—not because I'd left but because even before I did, you were never there to listen. You didn't see me, or hear me. But you were my whole world. And being so invisible to you, that you only saw me when you needed me…that was going to destroy me in the end, Seb. And I can't do that any more.'

Seb stepped fully into the room at last, reaching a hand out towards her, and Maria saw her chance to escape. She couldn't stay and talk about this. She just wanted to be alone.

Darting past him, she made for the door, but he wrapped an arm around her waist to stop her, holding her close—too close.

'Wait. Maria, please. Please, don't go, not like this.'

Maria wriggled to get free and he released his hold with a sigh. 'I'll email when I'm home,' she said, her words coming too fast. 'We can work out a visitation schedule for Frankie. I… I wasn't kidding about that—I want him to have you in his life. Although after today…'

'I'll make it up to him,' Seb said—automatically, it seemed. But it only made her remember all the times he'd said it before.

'You'll try,' Maria said wryly. 'You can't just buy kids off with more toys, you realise. He wanted *you* more than Santa.'

'I'll… I'll fix it, Maria, I swear.' He sounded so earnest, so desperate that Maria almost wanted to believe him. 'Look, between now and Christmas—no, now and New Year—I won't work at all. I fixed the contract thing with the Swiss team today. Everything else I can delegate! Probably. I'll sort it somehow. And it will just be you, me and Frankie for the next week, after Noemi and Max head to Ostania, and Leo and Anissa go back to New York. Just us. Our little family. Please. Just give me another chance.'

He still didn't understand, Maria realised. He never would.

It was a horrible echo of that last argument before she'd left. She'd told him he wasn't capable of giving her what she needed. Nothing had changed. And even worse, he didn't seem capable of even *understanding* what she needed. Of understanding the importance of love.

'This isn't something you can just fix, Seb. This is about who you are.' And who he was would never love her—let alone love her more than work. Living up to his father's legacy mattered too much to him.

'You're wrong. I can change. Look!' Without any more warning than that, Seb pulled his mobile phone from his pocket, strode to the window, yanked it open and tossed the device out into the snow. Then he turned to her, smiling proudly. 'See?'

Maria shook her head. 'I'm sorry, Seb. It's not enough.'

She turned, walked out of the office, and up the stairs to the room she shared with Frankie. Where, ignoring all the mostly packed cases and toys, she threw herself onto the bed and cried herself to sleep just as Frankie had done hours earlier.

It was over. For good this time.

Seb stared at the empty doorway for a long moment. And then he reached for the whisky bottle.

She loved him. Truly, deeply, properly loved him. The way his mother had loved his father. The way Leo loved Anissa and Noemi loved Max.

The way love was supposed to be.

The way he'd never imagined he'd get to experience.

He'd never told Maria, but it wasn't as if he hadn't thought about it over the years. The first time his father had raised the possibility of a union with his business buddy's daughter, he'd turned it down flat. He'd pointed out that Salvo had got to marry the love of his life. Why shouldn't he?

Except…there *was* no love of his life. No time to focus on anything but the business, being the success that Salvo expected him to be. And, honestly, most of the time the business was more fun than half the women he dated anyway.

Which had led him back to Maria, whom he'd last seen when she'd still been a teenager, two years younger than him and just an old family friend. But then she'd come home from university, twenty and poised and so, so beautiful…and he'd thought, why not? He had been twenty-two. His parents had been in love for years already by the time they'd been his age—hell, they'd even got married and had him by that point. Why wait for some mythical true love when he could marry the most beautiful woman he'd ever seen, make his father proud, save *her* father's business and inch closer to his long-term goal of taking over the company.

It had been everything he'd needed, all wrapped up in one gorgeous package. He'd have been an idiot to turn it down.

Finding out that Maria was still good company, and had seemed to be as attracted to him as he was to her…that had just cemented the fact that the marriage was a great idea. So he'd told his father yes, had bought a ring and gone through all the traditional motions.

And he'd known it wasn't love. He'd known

that Maria had had her own reasons for agreeing to the marriage—reasons that had nothing to do with how she'd felt about him. So he'd never let himself think about what it *wasn't*. Love had been off the cards for him—and how could he complain when he'd had everything else he wanted?

So he hadn't thought about love. Not once.

But now it was all he could think about. A question he had to find the answer to if he was ever going to fix this.

She loved him. She'd loved him since they were teenagers. Suddenly her answers about why she'd married him, from their night at the lake, rang false—or at least incomplete.

She'd said yes because she'd hoped he'd fall in love with her. But she'd never told him—so he'd never even considered it as a possibility. Had never *let* himself consider it.

Did he love her? He'd always loved her as a partner and friend. And he'd admitted to himself this week that she mattered more than *anything* in his world. That she was *everything*.

Was that love? The way she said she loved him?

He'd never even thought about it. Even after she'd left a year ago, he'd not considered it. He'd just assumed that eventually she'd come back to him. Like he'd told Leo, sometimes when you loved someone, you had to give them space. Because *of course* he loved Maria. He'd just never stopped to think about *how* he loved her.

Because she was already his wife, so what did it matter?

Except now it mattered. It mattered a lot. To her. And so it mattered to him.

Taking a long swig from the bottle, Seb tried to imagine waking up every day without Maria there. Tried to picture coming home without the promise of her to talk to about his day. It wasn't hard to do. He'd already lived it for the last year.

Then he shifted his focus. Pictured rushing home from work early just to spend time with her and Frankie—and maybe a younger sibling or two. Thought about crossing the hall from his office to hers at work to talk through the details of some deal or another. Considered that holiday they were going to take next year, just the three of them and the sunshine.

Most of all, he imagined kissing Maria good morning *every single* morning, and goodnight *every single* night. He thought about her happy, and realised with a shocked start that it was the only thing in the world he truly, desperately wanted.

Not the deal for the Swiss office, not the accolades and success for expanding the business, not Leo's shares in Cattaneo Jewels. Not even his father's approval, if he were still here to give it.

And that was the only thing he'd ever fought for before now.

Now he had a new fight.

He wanted Maria to be happy.

Just that. Just Maria, and, of course, Frankie. The two of them happy. If he had that, he didn't need anything else at all.

And that was his answer, right there.

Because he loved her. *Exactly* the way she loved him, even if it had taken him too bloody long to realise it. Even if he didn't behave like he did. Even if she didn't believe it.

He, Sebastian Cattaneo, was in love with his wife. And suddenly he understood a fundamental truth that his father had failed to teach him—probably because he'd thought it was too obvious to need to be said.

His family, and their happiness, was the greatest achievement he could ever hope to attain.

No other goal, objective or business plan could come close.

But it wasn't one he could achieve on his own. He needed help.

He needed people who had been down this hole before, and knew the way out. People who'd fallen so desperately in love and had found a way to make it work. To be happy together.

He needed his parents. But in their absence…

He reached for his phone, before realising

he'd already thrown it out of the window. Never mind—the person he needed most was already in the chalet. He just hoped she didn't mind a late-night wake-up call, especially since it was all for the highest of causes.

Seb stoppered the bottle and headed for the door, certain at last of what he needed to do next.

He needed to find his sister, and then his brother. And his brother-in-law-to-be and sister-in-law-to-be, come to that.

And probably a Santa suit.

Maria woke on Christmas Eve, bleary-eyed and sore-headed, to find Frankie clambering into bed beside her. As she snuggled his little body close, she tried to find the courage and energy to face the day ahead.

They were leaving. In just a few hours she and Frankie would be on their way back to that little cottage on her parents' estate in Italy, ready to spend Christmas together, just the two of them.

And she was glad about that. Really.

Glad that she'd made a decision at least. Glad that she wasn't going to spend the rest of her life waiting for Seb to wake up and see the woman he'd married. Glad that she could look to her future and—

Oh, who was she kidding? She hated it. But that didn't change the fact that it was the right choice.

She'd asked for what she needed at last. Had opened up and given him the chance to be the husband she needed.

And he'd thrown his phone out of the window instead. As if that equalled all the 'I love you's she'd never hear from him.

'Come on, *piccolo*,' she said, nudging Frankie to sit up. 'Let's go and find your aunt Noemi for a last play before we have to go home.'

Frankie nodded sleepily—apparently he hadn't been entirely awake when he'd crawled into her bed. He snuggled some more with his fox while she got washed and dressed, then decided that Frankie could stay in his pyjamas a little while longer at least. She listened at the door to make sure that Seb wouldn't be waiting to ambush her. Then, satisfied that he was either still asleep or had already left for the office, she led Frankie out and down the main stairs of the chalet, heading for the kitchen.

Only to stop and stare as they reached the top of the flight of stairs to the ground floor.

Beside her, Frankie gasped, clasping his hands together and looking up at her with wide eyes, before turning his attention back to the scene below again.

There, beneath the giant Christmas tree with all its glistening ornaments and lights, was a pile of presents in shiny wrapping paper. And standing next to the presents was—

'Santa!' Frankie cried, looking completely overcome by the whole situation.

Maria didn't blame him. But Leo in a Santa suit wasn't what was surprising her most about the whole tableau.

That was Sebastian in an elf costume next to him, with Anissa in a matching girls' version, while Max and Noemi both wore headbands with reindeer antlers. She almost didn't want to know what Seb had held over his siblings and sister-in-law-to-be and brother-in-law-to-be to get them to take part in this. Especially since it had been gone midnight when she'd walked out on Seb, and it was barely six in the morning now.

Apparently Seb really could pull off anything he set his mind to. He'd promised to make it up to Frankie, and he was. This was basically the dream, and a lovely way to finish the trip, since they wouldn't be there for actual Christmas Day tomorrow. This was fine—if utterly bizarre.

And it didn't change her decision one bit.

'Can I, Mamma?' Frankie asked, and she nodded, watching as he skipped down the stairs towards Santa. He stopped a few steps away as he recognised Santa's chief elf, though.

'Papà?' he asked, baffled.

Seb crouched down beside him. 'That's right,

Frankie. I'm so sorry I wasn't here to take you to meet Santa yesterday like I promised.'

'Santa's here now, though?' Frankie glanced between the elf that was his *papà* and the man in the big red suit with the white beard next to him.

'That's right, Frankie,' Leo said, in a suitably booming Santa voice, the beard disguising him well enough to fool a two-year-old. 'Your *papà* told me how sorry he was, and how much you wanted to meet me, so I made a special trip back to be here this morning—and made him promise to help me by being my special elf for the day. Now, how would you like a present?'

That was, of course, the magic word. As much as she'd told Seb he couldn't just bribe kids with toys, they weren't exactly likely to turn them down either.

Leo picked up the first parcel next to him, one with bright green shiny paper, and handed it to Frankie—who was almost the same size as the box. Max and Noemi both darted in to help him and Maria thought, not for the first time, how lucky their twins would be to have them as parents. Prince or not, she could tell how much Max loved Noemi, and how much effort he would put into always being there for her.

Which thought, of course, drew her back to Sebastian, who stood beside Frankie—but his eyes were on her. As soon as she looked his way, he took a step towards her, obviously wanting to continue their conversation from the previous night.

Maria shook her head, hoping he got the hint. There was nothing he could do now to change her mind anyway.

But then Santa looked up, too, a large envelope in his hand. 'Now, Frankie, it looks like this present is for your *mamma*. Would you like to give it to her?'

Frankie, engrossed in the toy train set he'd just unwrapped, shook his head. 'Papà do it.'

With a smirk that twisted his fake beard up, Leo handed the envelope to Sebastian, who smiled. So did Noemi and Max. And Anissa.

Oh, Maria didn't like how this was going one little bit.

'Why don't you take it into the other room to open it?' Noemi said, gesturing to the doorway to the snug with her antlers and giving Seb a little push in that direction, so Maria had no choice but to follow if she wanted her present.

She wasn't at all sure that she wanted her present.

But Frankie wanted her to open it. 'Go on, Mamma. I stay here with Santa.'

Okay, then. 'I'll be right back,' she promised.

Then she followed Seb into the next room, feeling suspiciously like she was heading into the lion's den.

CHAPTER FOURTEEN

SEB HELD THE door to the snug open for Maria as she walked through it, rehearsing what he wanted to say one last time. He hadn't slept in over twenty-four hours, he was dressed as a freaking elf, but, heaven help him, he was *not* going to mess up what had to be his last-ever chance to win his wife back.

Maria turned to face him, leaning against the back of the small sofa in the snug. 'Seb, look, this was a nice gesture for Frankie. And I appreciate it. I do. But I think we said everything we needed to last night, don't you?'

'No,' Seb disagreed. 'You may have done, but I have a lot more to say. Starting with this.' He held out the envelope on which Noemi had stuck a giant bow, even as she'd nagged at him to tell her what was inside. He hadn't, and Leo—the only one who knew about the contents by necessity—had kept his secret.

He wanted Maria to know this first.

She took the envelope gingerly, staring at the garish bow. 'You know, Seb, you can't buy me with gifts either.'

'I swear to you that is not what I'm trying to do.' Although now he thought about it rationally—or as rationally as he could after so little sleep—it could definitely look that way. 'Just…open it. And then let me explain, please. Okay?'

Maria nodded and peeled off the bow. Seb held his breath as she lifted the flap and pulled out the thick, creamy paper inside. 'This is another contract?'

'Not exactly.'

Her eyes widened as she read through it. 'This is…this is a controlling share of Cattaneo Jewels. You're giving me Leo's shares?'

'Well, Leo is, as soon as he's allowed to. Once it goes through, the family business will be more yours than mine.'

'Why…why would you *do* that?' she asked, exasperation leaking out in her tone. 'Seb, I told you, you can't buy me back. That's not what I want. I just—'

'You want to be free to find someone who loves you, the way my parents loved each other, the way Leo and Noemi have found someone, right?' Maria nodded, and Seb allowed himself a small smile. 'See, I do listen sometimes.'

'I know. And I appreciate this gesture, Seb. I do. And I know I'll always be in your life because we'll always have Frankie. But I don't need this. And I don't think… I don't think it would help, working so closely with you.'

'That was sort of the idea,' Seb muttered, and Maria's gaze turned suspicious.

'Wait, you gave me this to keep me here, didn't you? To buy me off. Because you can't give me what I *really* need—you don't love me that way. But you don't want anyone else to have me either, because I'm your *wife*. Seb, this is…this is low.'

'No!' Oh, hell, this was all going wrong. Very wrong. This was what happened when he planned a grand gesture on no sleep, clearly. 'That's not what this means, okay?'

Scrubbing a hand over his head—and dislodging his elf ears—Seb sank onto the sofa, his whole body aching with exhaustion. After a moment Maria sat down next to him.

'Okay, then. Tell me what it does mean. And why you're dressed up as an elf, come to that.'

Seb huffed a laugh. 'The elf thing was more for Frankie than you, unless you have some strange tastes you never mentioned before. And because Leo wouldn't wear the Santa suit unless I dressed up, too.'

'Ha! No. Although I think Anissa was secretly impressed with Leo's costume.'

'And she looks a lot better as an elf than I do,' Seb commented. Maria didn't disagree with him, which wasn't a surprise.

'So. Explain?' Maria asked. 'Everything, preferably. Starting from when I left you last night.'

Seb sighed. How to explain it in a way that she would believe? It felt like the realisation of his love had come on so slowly, over the years, then had sped up over the last week and a half. But would she believe that? If he just said 'I love you', Maria would think they were just words to make her stay, like she had with the shares.

It wasn't enough to just say the words. But he also knew the words were what would mean the most to her.

'When you left last night,' he started slowly, thinking his way through as he spoke, 'I realised that you were right about some things, and that I'd been dead wrong about others.'

'Like?'

'You said I didn't see you.' The memory was almost as painful as the words had been, especially when he knew what he'd been missing. 'And in lots of ways you were right. When we got married, I believed our relationship was one thing—a business deal, a partnership. And I never looked beyond that. In my head, I'd assigned you to the role of "wife of heir to Cattaneo Jewels", and looked forward to the day you'd be the "wife of the CEO of Cattaneo Jewels". And it never occurred to me to rethink that, until last night.'

'I noticed,' Maria said drily.

'But that doesn't mean that was all you were to me.' Seb twisted on the sofa so he was facing her, needing her to see the sincerity on his face. 'Just because I never assigned words to it the way you did, or even gave it too much thought… Maria, you were never just a convenience to me. You were a friend, a trusted confidante and partner, the mother of my child, and the most beautiful woman I've ever seen. With all those amazing qualities…of course I fell in love with you. So in love that you became an integral part of my life, and I'd jump through any hoop, meet any target you asked me to in order to keep you there. It just never occurred to me that, when you asked for those things, what you really wanted was my love. Because that was yours all along, even if I didn't realise it until now. I love you, Maria. Not as a friend or anything except as the woman I love. My wife.'

Maria froze, trying to take in his words. First Leo's shares, now declarations of love. Seb really was pulling out all the big guns to try to make her stay.

'Is this…? I have to ask. Are you just staying this to keep me here?' she asked, hating that it was even a question. But after everything…it was.

'No! Maria, I…' Seb stopped, looked down at his hands, then started again. 'You know what you said last night? About me being your first thought and last dream? I'd like to… Can I tell you about my day yesterday?'

His day? The day where he'd sneaked off to work in the early hours and skipped out on seeing Santa with their son? And he thought that was going to *help* his cause?

'I guess so,' she said, confused.

'I woke up yesterday morning to my phone buzzing, and all I wanted to do was ignore it and curl back up with you. But it wouldn't stop and I didn't want to wake you, so I checked my messages and…the deal my dad was working on before he died—the one you helped me work through the contract for? Well, you were right. That clause I dismissed…it was about to bring down the whole deal.'

'I told you so,' Maria said absently. Salvo's last deal. His legacy. Seb's last chance to make his father proud.

Suddenly Seb rushing off to Geneva to save it made a lot more sense.

He *had* been thinking about family, just in a different sort of way. And living up to his father's expectations had always been what had mattered most to him.

'It was…it was what Dad had been working towards for years. Our biggest expansion yet. He always said that once it was sorted, he was going to hand the whole company over to me and retire.'

'Only he never got the chance,' Maria murmured.

'Exactly. And I couldn't… I just couldn't let this one go down without a fight. You know?'

Maria nodded. 'So you went to Geneva.'

'I had to take a—a helicopter.' Seb's voice almost broke on that word. 'And I couldn't stop thinking about my parents, or what had happened to them. And I was just praying I could make it through and get back home to you, because I knew everything would be okay then. I was thinking of you and of Frankie the whole way there. How much I wished I was here with you. Or that you were there with me, distracting me, holding my hand, anything. I just wanted you there. No one else. Only you.'

Maria bit her lip. 'When I realised you must have taken a helicopter… I wished I could have been with you, too. But it didn't even occur to you to ask me to go with you.'

'How could I?' Seb asked. 'I was disappearing to take care of work stuff on our Christmas holiday. I mean, I'd forgotten all about Santa, I'll admit, but even so, I knew I was cutting it close with the rules and regulations you'd set.'

'*That* was why you didn't ask me?' Not because he hadn't thought of her, or because she wasn't important to him, but because he'd thought that was what she wanted. Because she'd set impossible rules that he couldn't help but follow.

Something, somewhere had got very messed up in their marriage.

'Yeah. Of course. Why else?' Seb looked at her, confused. 'Anyway, I *really* wished you could have come with me when I arrived in Geneva. All these idiots were up in arms about this contract, and I just knew that if you were there to talk it all through with them we'd have had it sorted in half the time. You were always so great at making these problems that looked huge more manageable, and you made far better sense of that contract than I could.'

'I… It's just about breaking things down into what really matters.' Which was basically the opposite of what she'd done when she'd arrived at Mont Coeur. She'd given Seb some convoluted and taxing targets to meet, and had never stopped to focus on what really mattered most to her— whether he loved her. 'Once you get to the heart of what both parties really want, it's easier to figure out where there's room to manoeuvre.'

'Exactly,' Seb said, his voice soft. 'Anyway, by the time I flew home again, I was frustrated, exhausted, and all I wanted was to come home to you. To tell you about my day—and how it would have been better if you had been there with me. But then I realised about the Santa thing, and I just… I knew I'd failed. I'd spent my whole life trying to make my dad proud, and my whole day trying to salvage his last deal, and in the end it was going to cost me what matters most in the world to me. You and Frankie.'

What matters most. Not his father's legacy. Not Salvo's expectations.

Her. Their family.

A small, warm thing that felt a lot like hope started to unfurl in her chest.

'So you called Leo and asked him for his shares and a Santa suit. And he said yes.' Maria shook her head. 'Seriously, he has taken to brotherhood amazingly well.'

Seb laughed, then sobered quickly. 'Actually… Leo said something else last night, something that got me thinking.'

'Oh?'

'He said…maybe the expectations I was trying to live up to weren't mine to meet.'

Maria tilted her head as she looked at him. 'What do you think he meant by that?'

'I think… I never knew about Leo until Papà and Mamma were gone. But now that I do… I wonder if the…pressure I felt was more about Papà's guilt over losing Leo than what he expected from me.'

'Salvo couldn't live up to his own expectations as a father because Leo wasn't there for him to be a father *to*,' Maria said, thinking out loud. 'It makes a lot of sense, you know.'

Seb shrugged. 'Maybe. I don't know. I need to think about it some more. But sometimes I wonder if I was trying to be two sons rolled into one. If that was why I was never enough.'

Maria reached over to grab his arm. 'You were enough for them, Seb. Salvo and Nicole…they loved you, so much. Not as a replacement for Leo but for yourself.'

'I know.' Seb glanced away, then cleared his throat. 'But we were talking about last night.'

Maria let go. One emotional breakthrough at a time. If she stayed—*if*—there'd be time to deal with Seb's feelings about his parents later. 'You called Leo?'

'Actually, no. I couldn't call, because I'd thrown my phone out into the snow in some sort of misguided romantic gesture.'

Maria winced. 'Of course.'

'So instead I had to knock on Noemi and Max's door and get *them* to call Leo and Anissa, and by that point everyone wanted in on the *next* grand gesture and…here we are.'

'They all wanted to be part of it?' Maria asked, a little touched.

'They all want you to stay,' Seb replied. 'Not as much as I do, of course, but maybe close. Apparently I'm a lot nicer to be around when you're here. Plus they all love you, too. They're your family as much as they're mine.'

Family. Wasn't that what she'd wanted when she'd married Seb in the first place? To have a place she belonged, where she was loved? And it was definitely what she wanted for Frankie, more than anything.

And she could have it if she stayed. If she trusted that Seb was telling the truth when he said he loved her.

She knew they couldn't be happy the way they had been before, and while the last week and a half had been better, it still wasn't what she really wanted from a marriage. She didn't want to have to hold her husband accountable to quotas and objectives every day of their lives. But she didn't want him to get so consumed with work that he forgot about them again either.

Which meant they needed a new plan. A new negotiation.

Starting with what mattered most this time.

Starting with love.

'If I stay,' Maria started, and Seb felt his heart rise, light with hope. '*If.* If I stay…we need a new plan. Not a contract or objectives like before,' she added quickly.

'Good. Because… I want to be the husband you deserve, and the father Frankie needs—really I do. And I want you to tell me what you need that to be. But I'd rather it happen because we're a team, working together to get where we want to go. Not because we both have our separate objectives to meet or we're going to fail.'

He'd spent too much of his life afraid of failing already. Too much of his life not being the son his father had given away, and not being good enough to make up for that loss.

Now he wanted to focus on being happy instead. On making Maria and Frankie happy, every single day.

'A team.' Maria smiled at him. 'That's what I want, too. You and me against the world. Well, you, me and Frankie.'

'Exactly. Plus… I've been thinking about this a lot lately, especially since we found out about Leo,' Seb said. 'I think… I think the only way to fail at being a family is to stop trying. As long as we want to be together…'

'And I do.' Maria grabbed hold of his hands suddenly, and Seb was surprised to see that there were tears in her eyes. 'That was always the problem, you see. I wanted to stay so badly. But I knew that if I stayed as things were, I'd never be happy. But now…'

'Now I'll make it my life's work to keep you happy. That's my only objective,' Seb promised. 'But… I'm going to need some promises from you, too.'

'Yeah?' Maria raised her eyebrows at him. 'Objectives? Goals?'

'I like to think of them as…vows. New wedding vows for us both. What do you think?' He barely remembered what he'd promised the first time round—he'd been too busy staring at how beautiful Maria was in her bridal gown, and feeling the gazes on the back of his head of the hundreds of people their mothers had insisted on inviting.

But this time…this time he knew the vows they made would stick with him through the years. That he'd think of them every morning, and live by them every day.

Even if there was no one else there to hear them make them, and he was dressed in an elf suit rather than a tuxedo.

These were the vows that mattered.

'Vows,' Maria said, with a smile. 'I like it. So, what were you thinking? You want to promise to love, honour and obey me?'

'Ha! No. You didn't even promise that last time.' He frowned. 'Did you?'

'Of course I didn't,' Maria said, rolling her eyes. 'But what, then?'

'How about… I promise to always keep you first in my heart, and in my mind?'

'I like that one.' Maria shifted closer, and he lifted an arm to place it around her, stroking her shoulder gently. 'And I promise to always tell you what I need, and let you find a way to meet that need. I think that sounds better than goals and targets, don't you?'

'Much,' Seb agreed. This was progress. But then his hand stilled on her shoulder. Next was the hardest one. 'And speaking of needs… Maria, I need you to promise not to run again. If things get hard, or I'm not being what you need, talk to me first. Please. I can fix anything if you stay long enough to let me. But the thought of what would have happened if you'd been able to get a flight out before I got back from Geneva…' That would have been the end of them. The end of this. Seb shuddered at the thought of it.

'I won't run.' Maria twisted and knelt up on the sofa, taking his face between her small, soft hands. When he looked into her eyes, he saw nothing but love, and marvelled again at how he'd never seen it before. 'I promise you, Seb. No, I vow. From here on, no running. We stick together and we work through things as a team.'

'That's all I need from you,' he replied.

Maria grinned. 'Then I think it's about time I got to kiss the groom.'

With that, she leaned in and brought her lips to his, soft and loving and for ever.

And at last Sebastian felt the knot around his heart loosen, and he knew that everything would be all right from now on. Just as long as they were together.

'Wait!' Maria said suddenly, pulling away from the best kiss of Sebastian's life.

'What?' he asked, panicked. They'd come so far. What else could there possibly be to keep them apart now?

But Maria was already on her feet, crossing the room to the fake bookcase, moving it out of the way and opening the safe.

The contract. Their first misguided attempt at fixing their marriage. Of course.

Maria shut the safe again, and brought the thick signed document towards him. 'Do you want to tear it up, or shall I?'

'I've got a better idea,' Seb said, taking it from her.

With one last look at the document that had almost saved—and almost destroyed—his marriage, Seb tossed it unceremoniously onto the fire.

'Now,' he said, gathering Maria back into his arms, 'where were we?'

'Right about here,' Maria said, and kissed him.

CHAPTER FIFTEEN

IT WAS ANOTHER half an hour or so before Maria and Seb emerged from the snug. She almost dreaded to think how many presents Frankie would have opened by now, but she just couldn't bring herself to tear herself away from her husband's arms now she'd found her way back into them at last.

He loved her. Truly loved her.

Time would tell if they could find a balance with the rest of it, but she was hopeful—which was something she hadn't been in a long time before this week.

'I gave you Leo's shares not as a bribe,' he'd explained between kisses, 'but so we could have a real partnership. Working together as well as playing together. I figured that way we're always on hand to remind each other of what really matters most when we get lost in the business.'

And he was right. What she'd wanted all along had been a more equal partnership, and now she was getting one. Their lives would no longer be separate, kept apart by work commitments and a family model that didn't suit them or their family.

They'd be a real team. And together she was sure they could take on the whole world.

Outside, under the Christmas tree, Leo, Max and Frankie had set up the most complex wooden train track Maria had ever seen. It snaked all the way through the large open-plan living area, with a bridge over a coffee table, before heading back through to the hall and looping round the tree. At some point Leo had clearly excused himself to change out of the Santa suit, but Max was still wearing the antlers, much to Maria's amusement.

Frankie sat, still in his pyjamas, right in the centre of the whole mess, watching his uncles push tiny wooden trains around the track and making train noises.

It was pretty much perfect.

'Aren't you glad you stayed to see this?' Noemi handed Maria a cup of coffee as she and Anissa came closer to watch the boys playing with their toys. Seb, Maria noticed, was already adding a side track with a turntable and another bridge.

'I am, actually,' Maria admitted, unable to hide her smile.

How close had she come to missing all this? By running the first time then trying to run again yesterday? If there had been a flight out then, she might have never seen Frankie playing trains with his uncles. Might never have known that Seb loved her.

If that wasn't a good enough reason to stop running when things got hard, she didn't know what was.

Noemi arched her eyebrows. 'So? Is all well in Maria Land? Do we get our final Christmas miracle after all?'

Maria watched as Seb knelt down to help Frankie set up a small forest of tiny wooden trees off to one side of the track. One by one, they methodically laid out the models, and every time Frankie knocked one over Seb would patiently pick it up and start again.

For a moment Maria couldn't help but see one or two more little people there with Seb. A whole little family, with siblings that Frankie could rely on and call for help, the same way Sebastian had today. Her future, in one perfect image.

Noemi was right. It was a Christmas miracle.

'Do you know, I think we just might,' Maria said, her eyes still on her little family.

Noemi and Anissa both gave a small celebratory whoop and clinked their coffee mugs together, making Maria smile even wider. She looked away at last, and turned to the women who were, to all intents and purposes now, her sisters.

'Thank you, both. For everything.' She pressed kisses to first Noemi's cheeks and then Anissa's. 'I know Seb couldn't have pulled this off without the two of you, and Max and Leo. And it's meant so much to Frankie.'

'I'm glad,' said Anissa.

'But you know we didn't just do it for him, right?' added Noemi.

'I know.' Maria ducked her head, warmth coming to her cheeks.

'If there's one thing I've learned over the last six months, it's that when times get hard, you need your family behind you. Whether they're blood relatives, or the people you grew up with, or just new friends who become family before you have time to even realise it.' Noemi was smiling at Max as she said that, Maria realised. 'Family is what matters.'

'And I can't tell you how happy I am to have mine back again,' Maria admitted.

'I'm just glad you found a way to get what you need, here, with Seb,' Noemi replied.

Seb fished under the tree for one last present, and handed it to Frankie. With a little help he unwrapped it to reveal a green wooden sleigh, just like the one she and Seb had ridden on, pulled by two reindeer with impressive antlers. 'Wow!'

He added it to the tableau of trees and trains with a proud expression on his face, then launched himself into his *papà*'s lap for a cuddle.

'Yeah,' Maria said softly. 'I think everything's going to be just fine.'

Christmas Eve, Seb reflected later, had been about as picture perfect as it could be. Between his new vows with Maria that morning, the relief of burning that bloody contract, Frankie's joy at Santa and his new train set, and just spending the day together as a family...it was all Seb had ever wanted. Tomorrow would be the more formal Christmas dinner—the whole family around the dining table for the first time since their parents had died (not to mention Leo's first time at a family Christmas dinner ever). But today had been...fun. Something Seb was starting to suspect had been sorely missing from his life for too long.

After a long afternoon of playing, Maria had swept Frankie away to eat something that didn't involve sugar, and Max and Anissa had gone with her. Max was apparently planning to make some sort of traditional Ostanian cocktail that sounded perfectly lethal, and Anissa had a secret supply of ingredients for making her grandmother's Christmas Eve cookies that she planned to bake and bring out to soak up the cocktails.

Which left just Sebastian, Noemi and Leo—the three Cattaneo siblings—sitting together under the lights of the Christmas tree, a small battery-powered train chugging slowly around the track surrounding them.

'So what was in the envelope?' Noemi asked, kicking her leg lazily over the arm of her chair. That was how she'd used to sit as a teenager, Seb remembered, and for a moment it sent him back in time—until he noticed the changes, showing how time had moved on. Her pregnancy bump was really on display at this angle, and Seb couldn't help but smile at the idea of his little sister as a mother.

He hoped she was half as happy as he was as a father. Looking at her, and watching her with Max, he was certain she would be.

He just wished their parents were there to see it. Still, he knew Nicole and Salvo would be proud of what they were all doing, and the choices they'd made—in their partners and in their futures. Even in the gift he'd given Maria that morning.

'Leo's share of the company,' Seb told his sister, and waited for the explosion.

Noemi bolted upright, at a speed that couldn't possibly be good for the babies. 'What?'

'I offered to sign my shares over to Sebastian as soon as I legally can,' Leo explained. 'I don't need them to feel a part of this family, and he knows the business better than I do.'

'That part I get. But… Seb? You gave them away—gave away the *controlling* share in our family business. To *Maria*?' Noemi's eyes were wide with amazement and…something else Seb couldn't put his finger on.

'Uh, yes. Are you…angry?' It seemed as good a guess as any. Maybe he should have talked to

Noemi first. Now they were getting along again, he really didn't want to ruin it so soon.

But Noemi laughed—high and tinkling and happy—and Seb's shoulders relaxed again. 'Of course I'm not angry! I think it's wonderful. You always loved that company more than anything...and now you love Maria most. That's exactly how it should be. I'm actually proud of you, big brother.'

'Well, okay, then. I'm glad you approve.'

'That said, though...' Noemi gave him and then Leo a calculating look. Then she nodded firmly, whatever decision she was working on clearly made. 'We should sign my shares over to you and Maria, too. I mean, I'm about to become a crown princess. It's not like I need the income. And to be honest...' she smiled, as if at a private joke '... I think I'll have enough wonderful things going on in my life as it is.'

'Well, if you're sure...' Seb said.

'I am.' Noemi glanced over at Leo, who hadn't said anything. 'And, actually, now is probably the perfect time to discuss that other thing I mentioned to you, don't you think, Seb?'

Now it was Seb's turn to grin. 'Absolutely.'

Leaning forward, Noemi twisted the ring on her right hand a few times until it popped off. Then she placed it in her palm and held it out to Leo, who stared at it, confused.

'It was our mother's engagement ring,' Seb explained, rather enjoying seeing his new-found brother dumbfounded for once. 'We want you to have it. For Anissa.'

'And before you start, it's totally obvious you're going to propose to her soon,' Noemi added. 'We think you should do it with this.'

'I… Well, yes. Actually, I was planning to… but I can't,' Leo said, shaking his head. 'This was your mother's ring. She left it to you, Noemi.'

'And I'm giving it to you.' Noemi placed the ring firmly in Leo's hand, then held on to his fingers for a moment. 'Listen. We have a lifetime of memories of our mother. I don't need a ring to remind me of her. But you missed out on all that. And this ring…it can't make up for that. But it can be that reminder for you.'

'Why would I need a reminder when I have you two?' Leo joked, but Seb could see the affection in his eyes. 'Thank you. Both of you.'

'Now you just need her to say yes,' Seb said, grinning at his brother. 'If you need them, I have some ideas about proposals…'

'Given that your last idea involved me dressing up in a Santa suit at six in the morning on Christmas Eve, I think I'll handle this one myself, thanks,' Leo said, smiling back.

Noemi shrugged. 'I don't know. I think Anissa liked the Santa suit…'

* * *

'"Merry Christmas to all, and to all a good night,"' Maria read, shutting the book quietly as the story came to a close.

Frankie was already mostly asleep on the bed beside her, lulled by the rhythm and rhyme of the classic festive story.

'He's had a long day,' Seb observed from the doorway. Then he yawned.

'Not as long as you have,' Maria replied with a low chuckle. The poor man couldn't have slept in thirty-six hours or more.

Tucking the blanket securely around Frankie, Maria placed the book back on the shelf and crossed the room to be wrapped in her husband's arms.

'Tomorrow we'll give him the most perfect Christmas,' Seb whispered in her ear, and Maria huffed a soft laugh.

'He already opened all his presents today.'

'Not all of them,' Seb muttered, and Maria rolled her eyes, even though he couldn't see her do it. Clearly, one of the things their team was going to have to discuss soon was not spoiling the children. Well, child for now. But maybe soon... 'We had to save some for epiphany. It's traditional.'

'Fair enough. And good call on the train track, by the way,' she said, to stop her mind running away with the possibilities of siblings for Frankie. 'He loves it.'

'I used to have one when I was little,' Seb said. 'Papà and I would play with it for hours.'

'And now you'll play with Frankie with his.' Maria thought about all the men playing trains that afternoon. 'And probably his uncle Leo and uncle Max, too.'

'He'll have so many people to love him,' Seb whispered. 'Even if his grandparents aren't here to see it.'

Tears stung Maria's eyes as she thought about how much Seb had lost this year. How much more she'd almost taken from him.

'Hey.' Seb tucked a finger under her chin and tilted it to make her look up at him. 'Don't cry. Things might not be perfect, but I know the future is going to be wonderful. Okay?'

'How do you know that?' Maria asked, dabbing at her wet eyes.

'Because I've found my Christmas miracle,' Seb said simply. 'You came home, and that was all I ever needed.'

Maria stretched up on tiptoe to kiss him, love burning bright in her heart.

'You're all I need, too. You, Frankie and me. Together.'

'Always,' Seb promised, and kissed her again.

CHAPTER SIXTEEN

ON CHRISTMAS DAY, just as Salvo and Nicole Cattaneo had hoped, all three of their children sat down around the huge dining table at Mont Coeur together, with their families and loved ones, to share a festive feast.

Before they tucked in, Sebastian got to his feet, wine glass in hand, and waited for the others to fall silent.

'I just wanted to say a few words before we eat, if that's okay?' he said, acutely aware that, really, as the oldest sibling, it was Leo's place to do so. But Leo was so wrapped up in his girlfriend— no, *fiancée* as of last night, it seemed—that it fell to Seb to say what mattered most.

As the others settled in to listen, Seb searched for the right words.

'This year has been a difficult one for all of us,' he acknowledged, watching as heads nodded around the table. 'We've lost our parents—in Leo's case, before he'd even got to know them. We've faced crises of confidence, business disasters and relationship issues. And there were so many times when any one of us could have given up on our families, on love, on our own happiness and just walked away.'

Leo wrapped an arm around Anissa's shoulders at that, pulling her close against him, a sign that he'd never let her go again.

'But we didn't. We fought on for everything that matters most to us. And it paid off for all of us. We each got more than we dreamed was possible as a result, and we're all here today to share our stories, and our Christmas dinner—just as Mamma and Papà hoped we would be.'

At that, Noemi leaned her head against Max's shoulder but reached a hand out to take Leo's. The brother they'd never known they had—and Seb already couldn't imagine ever being without him again.

'So today I'd like to thank you all for being part of my family. For knowing what I needed when I didn't. For supporting me when I needed it most. And for going above and beyond the call of family to help me fix the biggest mistake I ever made in my life—letting Maria walk away from me.'

Seb looked down and met his wife's gaze and held it, silently promising once more that he'd never let that happen again. He'd made his new vows, and he would keep them. However hard that was, and whatever happened next.

He knew what mattered most now. At last.

'But most of all, I'd like to raise a toast to absent friends.' Seb glanced up at the wooden ceiling, and imagined that if he looked hard enough, he could see his parents looking down on them all together. 'Mamma, Papà, we miss you. And I wish you were here today to see how far we've all come. I think you'd be very proud.'

Around the table, everyone raised their glasses. 'To absent friends.'

Seb sat down with a thump, the emotion of the day overwhelming him.

'Nice toast,' Maria said, pressing against his side. 'Your parents *would* be so proud of you, you know.'

'I hope so.' It had been so easy to say but harder to feel the truth of.

'I know so,' Maria said.

'Oh? And how is that?'

'Because I am.' Maria leaned across and pressed a kiss to the corner of his mouth. 'I'm so proud to call you my husband, Sebastian Cattaneo,' she whispered.

'Not half as proud as I am to have you as my wife,' he replied.

On the other side of the table, Noemi leaned forward, reaching around Leo to take Anissa's left hand and study the ring there.

'It suits you perfectly,' she said, beaming. 'Mamma would be so happy to see you and Leo engaged, you know. And Seb's right—she'd have loved to have us all here at Mont Coeur, together, for Christmas.'

'Not to mention preparing for a royal wedding next year,' Maria added, as Max placed a hand over his fiancée's baby bump, a reminder of the exciting future they had ahead of them.

Seb smiled at the thought of both his siblings happy and settled, though he just knew that they could never be as happy as he was to have Maria back in his life.

'Oh!' Maria jumped up suddenly. 'We forgot the cranberry sauce! Hang on.'

She dashed off to fetch it, and Seb watched her go. Then he spotted something hanging in the doorway between the dining hall and the kitchen.

'Dare I ask which one of you was responsible for that?' he asked, motioning to the mistletoe hanging there, waiting for unsuspecting couples to pass underneath.

Noemi shrugged her elegant shoulders. 'Well, at one point yesterday we really weren't sure if you'd need the extra help.'

'If I were you, I'd take advantage of it anyway,' Max said with a grin.

Seb considered, but only for a moment. And then he jumped up to wait for his wife under the mistletoe.

'We've got ordinary cranberry sauce or cranberry sauce with apple— Oh!' Maria gasped, as Seb caught her around the waist and kissed her thoroughly in the doorway, as Noemi whooped and even Leo gave a small cheer.

'Mamma! Papà!' Excited by all the noise, Frankie jumped down from his chair to join them. 'Frankie hug, too!' He wrapped his little arms around their legs, and Seb broke away, laughing, to embrace his son as well as his wife.

This Christmas was nothing like he'd dreamed it would be. But now it was here, he couldn't imagine it any other way.

All his Christmas wishes had come true. And Sebastian knew he'd appreciate the Christmas miracle that had brought his family together— all of them, even the brother he'd never known he had—all year long.

'Just think, next Christmas we'll have twins to add to the chaos,' Noemi joked, making everyone laugh.

But Seb just smiled, and placed a kiss on Maria's cheek as he ruffled Frankie's hair. 'Well, I for one can't wait. After all, Christmas *is* a time for family. Isn't it?'

* * * * *